BORN FOR THORTON'S SAKE

MARCIA LYNN McCLURE

Published by Distractions Ink
P.O. Box 15971
Rio Rancho, NM 87174

©Copyright 1996, 2005, 2007, 2012 by M. L. Meyers
A.K.A. Marcia Lynn McClure
Cover Photography by
©Konradbak | Dreamstime.com
Cover Design and Chapter Graphics by
Sheri L. Brady | MightyPhoenixDesignStudio.com

Third Printed Edition: 2012

McClure, Marcia Lynn, 1965—
Born for Thorton's Sake: a novella/by Marcia Lynn McClure.

ISBN: 978-0-9852807-1-0

Library of Congress Control Number: 2012934284

Printed in the United States of America

To Marnie,
*Thank you for your gifts of encouragement,
happiness and laughter,
and loyal, enduring friendship!*

$\mathscr{P}$ROLOGUE

"Where is she then? Where is the child?" Lord Richard Thorton demanded. "The girl was to have been here with you!"

The small, frail-looking woman trembled as she considered the three men standing before her. The dark and looming Lord Thorton's expression was no less than that of barely restrained fury. The expression of the dark and fine-looking younger man to his right was even more frightening. The third man, small and fair-haired, donned a pair of spectacles and seemed more disgusted than angry.

"What have you done with her then...madam?" the younger man asked. It was fully obvious this young man was Lord Thorton's son. Had it not been for the evident years between them, the two may have been mistaken for brothers.

The old woman swallowed hard, gathered courage, and stammered, "They...they assured me of being her only surviving relatives. I...I understood they...I...I understood they were in earnest." She breathed at last, glancing away from the faces of fury before her. She helplessly shrugged her shoulders when the man donning spectacles shook his head.

"You understood? Who are you to have understood anything, woman?" Lord Thorton bellowed. He placed a powerful hand at one temple and closed his eyes for a moment in an obvious effort to settle his temper.

"Father?" the younger man asked, placing a hand on Lord Thorton's shoulder. "Are you indeed well?"

Lord Thorton nodded and inhaled deeply as the woman wrung her hands nervously.

"Forgive me, sire. I thought it would be best if—" she began.

"No, madam. You did not think," Lord Thorton scolded.

His son began to pace back and forth, yet angry. "Is there an address?" he asked.

"No, sire. They just...they just took her," the woman answered.

Lord Thorton sighed with exasperation. "A name then, woman! Did you even think to get a name?"

The woman shook her head, brushing at the tears fresh on her cheeks. "No, sire. I assumed—"

"She is lost to us, sire," Jacob Peterson said quietly to his employer. He adjusted his spectacles and again shook his head disapprovingly at the old woman.

Deep concern crossed the face of the mighty lord, Richard Thorton, as he looked to his son Brockton.

"Yes, Peterson," the great lord mumbled. "Lost to us."

"For the time being, perhaps, Father," Brockton said. "But fear not. She cannot be lost to us long. She will not be."

Lord Thorton nodded in agreement with his son. "We will find her," he said. "I'll not let Charles Holt's daughter be lost indefinitely."

Lord Thorton lumbered away then, his son at his side, leaving their solicitor, Jacob Peterson, to contend with the sobbing proprietress of the orphan asylum.

"Madam," Jacob began, "please…do calm yourself." He reached into his pocket and produced a small calling card." Here is an address. If ever you hear from the couple who made off with the girl, do not, for any reason, hesitate to contact his lordship or myself. I am Jacob Peterson, Lord Thorton's solicitor." He paused and then added, "Forgive my employer and his son, madam. His lordship was deeply affected by the loss of the girl's father. The best of boyhood companions, they were." With a tip of his hat, Jacob Peterson exited, leaving the old woman still trembling in her slippers.

THORTON'S WARD

Maria was awakened by a furious beating at the cottage door. *Who could it be*, she wondered, *at this late hour?* Silently she rose from the pile of ancient quilts that served as her bed and crept from the dark loft to the door at the bottom of the stairs. Opening the door only a slice, for she knew better than to be caught milling about, she peered into the adjoining room. Her aunt and uncle, having left their chamber, grumbled and argued as they rather stumbled along together toward the cottage door.

"Who would dare disturb us at this hour?" Aunt Eula Holt complained, tightening her night robe about her and adjusting her nightcap. Her short, round husband followed her, cursing under his breath.

"Maybe that brat's out and about stirring up mischief," Edgar Holt growled. "Might as well drown children at thirteen years as put up with their nonsense."

"Well said," Eula grumbled, nodding her agreement.

The beating on the door suddenly increased in volume, causing Maria to startle slightly. She quickly forgot her uncle and aunt's spiteful remarks about her age and uselessness as her eyes widened in anticipation. What goings-on could cause someone to beat on the door in the dead of night? Robbers perhaps? Maria shook her head, knowing full well robbers would no sooner knock on a door than verbally shout out their intentions.

"Just a moment! Just a moment! We're coming!" her aunt screeched. Maria saw her aunt open the cottage door and heard her ask, "Who dares disturb us at such an hour? I hope you have good reason for..." The homely woman hushed, however, and Maria gasped as an enormous man suddenly burst into the cottage. The dark trespasser was followed by a small, thin man who wore spectacles. He nodded at her aunt and uncle in turn.

"Where is she, woman?" the tall, dark intruder growled.

Maria's aunt quickly regained her composure and shouted, "Who do you think you are...forcing yourself into our home as such?"

"Where is the girl?" the dark man demanded. "You had better cooperate with me, woman! Otherwise, this will go very badly."

The smaller man adjusted his spectacles and interrupted, "Is this indeed the residence of Edgar and Eula Holt?"

"Well…well, yes. But I still do not see why you think you can simply—"Eula began.

"Do you have residing here in your care one Miss Maria Castillo Holt?" the spectacled man inquired.

Maria tucked a strand of ebony hair behind one ear, her eyes widening, her heart pounding at the mention of her name. She held her breath, entranced as she watched the color drain from her aunt's face. Her uncle cleared his throat and with a raspy voice answered, "My niece. My brother's child. Yes. She lives here with us."

"Give her over to me at once!" the towering man shouted. Taking a clearly threatening step in her uncle's direction, he stopped when the spectacled man put a hand to his arm.

"Master Brockton, please," the spectacled man said to him calmly. Turning, the man in the spectacles handed Edgar Holt a small calling card and said, "My card. I am Jacob Peterson, solicitor for Lord Richard Thorton and his son Brockton. I have here the last will and testament of one Charles Victor Holt. The will states, without question, that in the event of his demise—being his beloved wife, Lucia Maria Castillo Holt, had previously departed this life—his only child, one Maria Castillo Holt, is to be placed in the home of Lord Richard Benton Thorton…he also being appointed sole guardian until such time as…in short, we've come to transport the child to her rightful guardian and residence."

"Let me repeat myself. Give the child over to me at once!" the larger man growled at Maria's aunt.

"Master Brockton, please," Jacob Peterson said quietly to his enraged companion.

The large man sighed heavily and turned from the others. The dim light from the lamp Maria's aunt carried illuminated his face then, and Maria gasped at the sight of him. She was very young, it was true, but even eyes as young and innocent as hers could recognize pure perfection of face and form in a man such as stood there in the cottage. Maria moved to cover her gaping mouth with one hand, causing the door to creak open a bit more. The almost inaudible sound arrested the man's attention, however. He stared then, frowning in the direction from whence it came.

"Oh, no! No, no!" Maria whispered to herself, panicked as he began striding in her direction.

"Master Brockton? Brockton? Sir?" Jacob Peterson called as he watched the son of his employer stride toward the door.

Brockton pulled the door open, and Maria stood unmoving staring up, up, up into the handsome but angry face looking down at her. A perplexed expression momentarily crossed the striking countenance of Brockton Thorton. Reaching out, he cupped the girl's chin in one strong and gloved hand.

"Peterson. She is here," he said, his tone somewhat softer than before.

"Now wait a moment." Eula Holt began walking toward them. "She is our charge! I'll not let you—"

"No, ma'am. She is not! She is the ward of my father...and she will be taken to my home this night!"

Brockton growled, still gazing down at Maria. Maria was entranced, her breath gone from her, her heart pounding like some furious drum. The pure essence of the man before her seemed to wash over her like a warm summer rain, and she could only stare up at him in awed silence.

"Edgar!" Eula shouted, turning to her husband.

Edgar Holt cleared his throat once more. "Sir, I am her uncle...blood relation. We will be keeping the girl."

Brockton Thorton ignored the man as he spoke to Maria. "Gather your things, girl. You'll not have to reside with these...degenerates any longer."

His voice was rich and low and sent a quiver of unfamiliar security erupting through Maria. She smiled warmly up at him, resisting the urge to throw her arms about his neck and embrace him thankfully.

His eyes narrowed and his frown softened as Maria spoke. "Do you mean to say...you're truly going to take me away from...from here?"

"I do. This very night, child," he assured her. Again, the sound of his voice caused Maria's breath to still for a moment. "Now...run and gather your belongings," he said.

Maria's eyes were alight with delight, and fearing she might still be unable to resist embracing him, she rushed past him, saying, "I've no belongings to gather, sir." Taking Jacob Peterson's hand in her own, she shook it vigorously and said, "Thank you as well, Mr. Peterson."

Maria smiled when the serious-faced, spectacled

man smiled at her. She mused smiles from a solicitor were rare, and she felt warmed by his smiling at her.

"Now…see here—" Eula began.

"Constable Henry is just outside, madam. If you would prefer to invite him in to add validity to our claim, I'm certain he will be more than happy to oblige," Jacob Peterson said firmly.

"She's just annoyed because she'll have to tend to the cottage herself and do her own washing now, Mr. Peterson," Maria whispered to him. "She does not really care if I leave. Thus…may we go now?"

"Yes, girl. We'll go now," Brockton replied, coming to stand next to her. His eyes traveled the length of her then, a frown puckering his handsome brow. "Yet surely you have a cape? A wrap? Something to warm you. The snow is heavy out."

"No. Just this," Maria said, motioning to the threadbare gray dress she wore. It was obviously too small. Brockton looked the child up and down once more, his eyes resting on her feet, which were wrapped in articles resembling what had once been shoes.

Suddenly, the young man lunged toward Maria's uncle as his anger exploded again. "You miserable…" he began, raising a fist. His intent was obvious: to let it go against the weak jaw of the fat, spineless man.

Edgar Holt doubled over to protect himself as Maria stepped between them. Looking up into the angry face of her defender, she smiled and said, "It's all right and good now. You and Mr. Peterson have come, haven't you?"

Jacob Peterson cocked one eyebrow, looking on in astonished wonderment as the powerful young man stared into the deep blue of the young girl's eyes.

"Yes. Yes, we've come," Brockton said, smiling, and lowered his fist. He turned to Peterson and chuckled, "She's an enchantress, I believe, Jacob."

Peterson smiled and nodded. "She would have to be to calm your anger thus, Master Brockton."

"I'll not let you take her," Eula argued. "Think of it…two men taking charge of a young girl. It's not proper, and I'll not have the country saying I allowed—"Aunt Eula began, feigning concern.

Maria again smiled at her handsome rescuer. "This man is a gentleman, Aunt Eula. Of course, you would not be expected to recognize that."

"Impertinent wench!" Eula gasped. "Take the little wretch then. Though I'd not wish her sharp tongue on even the likes of you!"

Brockton removed his heavy black cloak and wrapped it tightly around Maria. Effortlessly scooping her up in his arms, he strode to the door.

"Good evening," he growled, smiling acidly at the remaining occupants of the cottage. "Come along, Peterson. We have what we came for."

Maria glanced over Brockton's shoulder, watching her aunt and uncle as she was carried from their home. Oddly, she found herself offering a wave of farewell, a strange yet small pricking of sentiment in her heart. They were, after all, her blood relations. Yet as they simply lifted their noses in the air and closed the cottage door, Maria was reminded of how she would never miss them.

Brockton mumbled to Jacob, "Vile couple, I'll tell you that."

Maria looked into the perfect face of the man who carried her. What must he think of her eagerness to go so easily with him? "Thank you, sir," she began. "I'm certain you think me very ignorant to come away with you so willingly…but I'm assured nothing can be worse than living with them as I did."

"Astonishingly, innocence is still evident," Jacob Peterson said, shaking his head in disgust.

The scowl returned to Brockton's face as he said, "And I am thankful for it."

Maria chose to be silent, only partly understanding their inferences.

Opening the door to the coach, Brockton gently placed Maria inside. Moving aside, he allowed Peterson to seat himself first, following him into the conveyance. Maria was disappointed when Jacob sat next to her rather than the dashing Brockton. Yet she was safe and warm. Pursued, freed, and protected.

"Home then, Tom," Brockton shouted to the coachman. The carriage lurched forward, and Maria pulled Brockton's cloak more tightly around her. Even for the dark of midnight, the brilliance of the full moon allowed sufficient light into the coach, and Maria could not help but smile as she glanced quickly at her handsome rescuer.

"They've treated you badly, obviously," Brockton

suddenly growled. Maria shrugged and turned her face to gaze out the window into the moonlit night. "To what extent were you…mistreated, girl?" he asked.

Maria continued to stare out the window as she answered. And answer she did, for such a voice and such a man could not be dismissed.

"Merely neglected, sir…perhaps overworked. Resented, as well, I suppose. Yet nothing I'll not recover from quickly, I assure you."

Brockton released an angry breath and continued, "Were you aware your father had named my father as guardian to you?"

Maria ventured to look at him then, battling the tears threatening to escape her eyes. "If your father is Lord Richard Thorton…yes. My father spoke of him often. I thought…I thought…"

"You thought you were not wanted by my family," Brockton finished for her.

Maria nodded and returned her gaze to the night once again.

"Your aunt and uncle spirited you away before his lordship was able to locate you, Miss Holt," Jacob Peterson explained.

Maria only nodded, afraid her voice would reveal the true depth of her emotion if she spoke. She wiped a tear from her cheek.

"Are you indeed thirteen at this point, girl?" Brockton asked.

She nodded again, pulling the massive cloak more snugly about her.

"Well, then," Brockton continued, "this is Jacob Peterson, and I'm Brockton Thorton. My father, Lord Thorton, is extremely ill and was unable to attend to you himself. Please believe me when I tell you only illness as excessive as his could render him incapable of finding you. I hope I will suffice in his place. I assure you…you are more than wanted in our home. My mother will, no doubt, be beside herself with joy at the onset of your arrival."

"Lady Thorton is a wonderful, kind, and loving woman, Miss Holt. You'll feel quite at home with her," Jacob Peterson added reassuringly.

There was silence then. No one spoke until Jacob at last suggested, "Let's rest, all of us," he suggested. "The hour is late, and it is such a long way."

"You must indeed be tired, Miss Holt," Brockton said. "To be awakened as such in the dead of dark night. It would be wise to at least rest your eyes."

"Yes," Maria said, feeling disappointed somehow. "Yes, I suppose I am tired." Though how sleep would ever come she did not know. She had only just been liberated! And now she sat in a carriage with the most handsome man the heavens had seen fit to place on the earth, and she was expected to sleep? She was on her way to a new home, to meet with strangers! However did they expect her to slumber?

Yet inside the coach all was quiet as it moved rhythmically along. Before the quarter of the hour had passed, Maria was indeed deep in contented slumber.

❧

"She's a beautiful girl!" Jacob whispered, assured the girl slept.

"Yes," Brockton agreed, studying the sleeping miss. "I had heard stories of her mother's beauty. Still…I did not expect…she's only thirteen, after all."

"The blackest hair and bluest eyes," Jacob whispered. "The heritage of Spain is certainly apparent."

Brockton smiled as he watched his friend adjust his spectacles and examine the napping girl again. Brockton studied her a moment as well. He could only ineptly attempt to fathom what the child's beauty would be once she was a grown woman. Judging from that beauty that she already possessed, it would be unsurpassed.

Her lips were red and her mouth rather the shape of a heart. Thick, ebony, and exceptionally long lashes fluttered every now and again as she slept, hiding the brilliance of her eyes. Her hair was lush and long and held a bluish tinge, so black was it. The form of her figure was unsettlingly developed as well and further manifested evidence of the faultless, feminine contours that would be hers in matured womanhood.

"It is no doubt the woman resented her, Master Brockton," Jacob whispered as he continued his survey of the girl.

Brockton quietly chuckled. "I believe she's bewitched you, Peterson. I've never seen you stare at any person thus previously."

Peterson smiled, removed his spectacles, and began polishing the lenses with a handkerchief. "Yes. And noticeably…she's a sharp little chit in the parcel."

"And so it would seem," Brockton agreed, smiling as he closed his own eyes, resting his head against the back of the conveyance.

⚜

A rut in the road and the accompanying jolt of the coach awakened Maria. She looked about, momentarily forgetting where she was. Yet in a moment, her memories flooded her consciousness, and her eyes were drawn to the remarkable form of Brockton Thorton.

As Jacob Peterson snored quietly at her side, Maria could only stare at Brockton, awed as she considered him. She found his great height somewhat intimidating, but masculine all the same. She wondered at his age. Twenty and five years, perhaps? Surely at least twenty and two or three, for there was no mere boy possessed of such large stature and squared jaw. A straight and perfect nose to match the chiseled lines of his face, as well. Oh, he was a handsome man! Though his eyes were now closed, Maria remembered their deep, mapled brown. His dark brows and eyelashes and perfect painter's-portrait mouth were visible, and she smiled at the sight of them before her. Her smile broadened as she thought of this epitome of masculinity exposing one charming dimple at his left cheek when he had first smiled at her. The dimple lent a touch of boyhood to his otherwise wholly mature appearance, and she liked it best of all his features. As she studied him further, she noted his hair was exceedingly unusual in its tint. For the most part it was brown, but now and again a fleck of gold appeared midst the abounding chestnut. Maria thought it charming in its distinctiveness. Suddenly pulling her gaze from him, she felt herself blush. She wondered if her mere thirteen years and dependent circumstances named her attraction to Brockton Thorton exceedingly "inappropriate."

In an effort to distract herself, she turned her attentions to the man next to her. Instantly she smiled. What contrast! Jacob Peterson was not a handsome man in the least of it. Maria thought him somewhat cute, however—like a puppy newly birthed. Yet for all his stiffness and severity, he was pleasant. He owned thin, very fair hair, barely a line for each lip, and a rather unfairly pronounced nose. Maria continued to smile all the same. She knew she was much better off in the care of the two men with whom she shared the carriage than living with her uncle and aunt. Surely life would be happier, full, and carefree in the home of Lord Thorton.

Closing her eyes once more, Maria tried to imagine a new life—a life filled with warm hearths and those who had been friends to her parents. A life filled with a thing so wonderful as Brockton Thorton to gaze upon every day.

※

The halting of the carriage woke Maria once again, and she blushed as she found Brockton studied her unwaveringly. He did not look away until the coachman opened the door.

"At last. I'm as stiff as a corpse," he grumbled, stepping out of the carriage.

"Thorton Manor, Miss Holt. After two years, you are home at last." Jacob exhaled, adjusting his spectacles and smiling warmly at her. He stood down from the coach, and Maria began to follow.

"Only wait. The mud is deep here," Brockton said as he glanced around at the ground. Maria gasped as he took her hand, pulling her from the carriage and into the cradle of his arms. As he turned, Maria's mouth gaped in astonishment as she saw, for the first time, the beautiful grandeur of Thorton Manor. It was a vast and wonderful work of stone with four high-reaching turrets and a lovely dressing of ivy vine. The windows glowed warm, an enchanting invitation through early morning shadows.

As Brockton carried her toward the manor house, a beautiful and elegant woman came fairly floating down the steps to meet them. She was a tall woman, with hair the unique tints of Brockton's.

"Oh, Brock! Darling, you've found her! You've brought her to me!" the lovely woman called. The woman was undeniably Brockton's mother, for Maria noted she bore a dimple on one of her own cheeks.

"Yes, Mother. Indeed, I've brought you a girl to primp and pamper and dote over. Now, let us in. We are chill-bitten and voracious," he chuckled.

"Of course! Oh, of course," Lady Thorton cooed.

"Darling! You must be frozen through and through," she said to Maria.

"No...no, milady. I...I am quite well," Maria stammered, feeling all the more abhorrent of her appearance than ever she had before.

"Well, darling...we'll warm you straight away," Lady Thorton said softly. Her smile was like sunshine, and Maria felt glad to be near her.

Once inside the manor house, Brockton let Maria's feet fall to the floor, and she quickly curtsied to his mother.

Lady Thorton's eyes widened with delight. "Oh, Brock, darling...she's simply enchanting! The very image of her mother!"

"So I gathered," Brock muttered.

"The very image! Hello, Maria," Lady Thorton said quietly, extending her hand toward the girl. "I'm Emeline Thorton...Brock's mother."

Maria tentatively offered her own hand, expecting the woman to grasp it in welcome and release it. Instead, Lady Thorton clutched Maria's hand tightly and enticed the girl nearer with her maternally entrancing smile. Drawing in her breath, Lady Thorton donned an expression of utter joy. Looking past Maria to her son, she said, "Lovely, Brock. Isn't she?"

"Yes, Mother. She's adorable," he chuckled. "No doubt we'll need an entire room for the wardrobe Mother has in mind for you, girl."

Maria smiled, feeling as if warm syrup were being drizzled into her mouth as she gazed up into Brockton's face as he smiled at her. The dimple in his cheek was entirely charming.

Maria looked away from Brockton, her eyes widening in surprise as Lady Thorton suddenly squealed with delight. "Oh! I'm so happy to have you here with us at last! Lord Thorton, my husband, will want to see you the moment you've eaten and rested. It is all too exciting!" The ecstatic woman smiled at her son, fairly beaming resplendent joy.

"Now, Maria, let's go up and draw a warm bath for you. Then…I cannot wait to get my hands in that hair of yours!" Lady Thorton giggled. Taking hold of Maria's hand, she led Maria toward a high winding staircase.

Maria paused, however, and, turning to the two men who stood watching, said, "Thank you. Thank you both for your trouble. How can I ever—"

"Do not trouble yourself with thanks. For no doubt the day will come when you may regret…" Brockton began, his smile fading, the charming dimple in his cheek disappearing all at once.

"Thank you, Miss Holt. For trusting us," Jacob Peterson finished.

Maria almost frowned, puzzled by Brockton's response to her thanks. Still, donning a grateful smile, she allowed Lady Thorton, chattering excitedly all the while, to lead her along up the stairs.

"Perhaps we should not have sought her out…delivered her. Perhaps, Peterson, we should have left her there. When the day comes…when she's told…" Brockton muttered, watching his mother lead the girl up the staircase.

"Not to worry, Master Brockton. When the day comes, I believe she will bless it," Jacob said. He patted the young man on the shoulder and turned to seek out the father. Lord Thorton must be informed of a task fulfilled.

RETURNING

Nearly three years had passed since the blessed day Maria arrived into the loving care of those who dwelt at Thorton Manor. Three years filled with love, joy, and treasured companionship, three years in which Maria had lived happily secure and without worry.

Lord Richard Thorton had wept when first he set eyes on Maria the night Brockton and Jacob Peterson delivered her to the manor house. He spent hours apologizing to her for the time wasted and for being so long in finding her. He often spoke of her father and the deep friendship they had shared. The great Lord Richard Thorton passed away only one year after Maria's arrival at Thorton Manor. She had mourned him as deeply as she had her own father at his passing.

Brockton then inherited the title, lands, and all else that had been his father's, including his responsibilities to his father's ward, Maria. And yet even with his frequent absences due to duty and business, Brockton always set his ward as a priority. Brockton taught Maria to ride and to play cards, helped her to improve her dance. On her fourteenth birthday, Brockton himself gifted Maria her beloved chestnut mare, Valerian. Ever and always Brockton was the stone, the foundation in Maria's life. Even though he was nearly six years her elder, in Maria's mind he had fast become her greatest friend. All the while he was attending her, she knew he must at times grow weary of her. Yet he masked his boredom or weariness, seeming thoroughly content with her company. And Maria valued nothing above Brockton, Brock as he was known to her then. He was her joy, her security, her confidant, and, secretly, the vital craving of her heart, mind, body, and spirit. Brock Thorton had become breath to Maria Castillo Holt. A breath she knew could never be entirely respired.

Thus three years passed, and in three weeks Maria was to reach sixteen. Arrangements had been ongoing for months in preparation for her coming-out. Brock would be returning from the business that had kept him away for nearly three months to attend the event, and Maria thought she might die of the anticipation of his arrival.

Maria had been restless the entire day, constantly attempting to discover methods of entertaining herself as the minutes ticked until he arrived. She had ridden Valerian early and very long in the morning, helped old George in the gardens, and baked bread with Matty in the kitchens, and still Brock was not expected for hours.

As Maria paced anxiously in the library, Lady Thorton chuckled. "It won't be much longer, peach. He'll be riding up at any moment."

"I loathe the waiting. It seems ages since he was last here," Maria sighed, smiling achingly and kneeling at the woman's feet.

Lady Thorton cupped the beauty's face in her hands. "You've been happy here, haven't you, darling?" she asked, her expression suddenly serious.

Maria frowned, puzzled. "Oh, ever so blissfully happy! How could you doubt it?"

Lady Thorton sat back in her chair and sighed. "And Brock. He is dear to you, isn't he, Maria?"

Maria laughed. "Of course! Dearer than anything!"

The grand mistress of Thorton Manor seemed relieved. "Yes. I can see it. I don't know why I worry so." Maria frowned and shook her head, puzzled. Lady Thorton had not been entirely happy since her husband's death, and it saddened Maria to see her worry.

Maria stood and kissed the woman affectionately on the cheek. "I'm going up to my chamber. Maybe I can occupy myself somehow. I just loathe this waiting!" Maria made her way up the winding staircase, humming to herself as she walked to her chamber.

Once there, she sat at her window, gazing out into the beauties of new spring. Yet her anxieties began to whisper in her mind. She felt grateful Lady Thorton had not seemed to sense the actual depth of her feelings for her son, Brock. Maria had only recently admitted silently to herself how deeply in love with him she was. However, she had become skilled at giving the appearance of mere friendship with Brock, while in reality the fact of it nearly broke her heart.

But she was a sensible girl. Brock was much older, and now he had the title and the properties to pass on. No doubt the day would come—and all too soon—when he would marry. At the thought, Maria's hand encircled her throat as she fought the constricting sensation beginning there. Each pulse of her heart offered her an odd pain. She swallowed hard, tried to push the musings to the back of her mind. Yet there was more to breed anxiety, for she was to have her coming-out in a matter of weeks! Then what? Would she have suitors? And Brock, being now her guardian—would he be the one to give her over to those who wished to court her? She couldn't think of it! She wouldn't.

She heard it then: the unmistakable rhythm of Stetson's gallop approaching. She leaned through the open window to watch him ride in, tears filling her eyes as he approached. Brock glanced up and caught sight of her. A smile instantly spread across his face, his beloved dimple creased one cheek, and he waved.

"Brock!" Maria couldn't help calling out his name; the feel of it was pure confection to her lips.

Brock reined Stetson to a halt just beneath Maria's window. "Hello! Have you missed me?" he called, still smiling and looking up at her.

Maria only smiled through her joyous tears, vigorously nodding her assurance.

"Oh, you simply like the gifts and trifles I bring back for you," he said, reaching into his saddlebag and withdrawing a package. He tossed it up to her and smiled as she caught it.

"It's for your coming-out! I chose it with that in mind. Now, come downstairs and meet me." With another mesmerizing smile, he signaled Stetson and rode off toward the stables.

Maria tossed the package onto her bed and stood before her looking glass. "Oh. I'm so...so..." she grumbled. She smoothed her hair and pinched her cheeks to blush them, though it was hardly necessary, for Brock brought a blush to her cheeks easily enough.

Maria left her chamber, resigned to descend the staircase slowly and elegantly to greet him this time, instead of in the impatient leaps and bounds as were her standard. After all, she was a young woman now.

However, when she had descended half the distance of the staircase, Brock entered through the main door. Maria was overcome with excitement, springing at him as a happy sparrow. He caught her in his wonderfully familiar embrace as she threw her arms around his neck.

"You're home! You're home," Maria whispered into his ear. She could feel Brock's roughly shaven face nuzzle her neck, and she hoped he wouldn't notice the goose flesh breaking over her because of it. Her senses were overcome—thoroughly and entirely overcome! She found her body trembled, within and without, her mouth watered, and her breathing was labored. Oh, how she loved him—loved the scent of him, the feel of his cheek against hers, the power of his arms around her! Another moment and she would be undone, confessing her true feelings for him aloud.

He held her gently away from himself, his eyes narrowing as he grinned rather mischievously at her. "What? Tears?" he asked then, his own eyes brilliant with overabundant moisture.

"You've been gone so long this time," Maria whispered. As he pulled her into his powerful embrace once more, she fancied for a moment the young lord of the manor could no longer hold her at bay. She fancied he felt her a soft, tempting, fragrant beauty. She fancied he did not want to further deprive himself of the blissful sensation of having her in his arms. But these were only fancies, and she knew it.

Still, she clung to him tightly, drinking in the scent of his hair and skin, the sense of his proficient embrace as his muscular arms locked her forcefully in their binding strength. Absolute exhilaration reverberated throughout Maria as Brock nestled his face against her neck, causing her to tremble as the sensation of his hot breath on her flesh heated her soul with ravenous fervor.

"Maria," he whispered, and she gasped quietly at the extreme emotion evident in his voice.

The ardent enchantment threatening to consume her immediately evaporated as Maria opened her eyes, catching sight of the beautiful woman entering through the front door. Releasing Brock, Maria stepped backward and out of his beloved embrace.

"Maria?" he asked, a puzzled frown puckering his brow.

"Hello. You must be little Maria," the woman said, approaching with the grace of a great lady indeed.

Brock turned to look at the other woman and said, "Oh. Maria, this is Rebecca Dellancy. And, Rebecca, this is my...this is Maria."

"Hello," Maria managed, bending a respectful curtsey.

"Rebecca has come for a visit until her—"Brock began.

"I've heard so much about you, Maria!" Rebecca interrupted. "Brock talks of you endlessly. And I've never known a man to spend so much time and consideration on purchasing a—oh! I almost forgot. It's to be a surprise for her coming-out, is it not, Brock, darling?"

Maria took several more steps backward. She felt ill and close to fainting. "I'm...I'm sure your mother will want to see you immediately. I'll let her know you have come home," she stammered. Turning, she walked to the library as calmly as she was able.

"She seemed quite overjoyed to see you home, Brock," Maria heard Rebecca giggle in a hushed tone.

Was it upon her then? All she had come to fear, Brock's necessity to take a wife—was the loathsome nightmare upon her? So soon?

"He's home," Maria stated upon entering the library.

"Is he?" Lady Thorton exclaimed. She seemed to

immediately note the lack of color and the expression of utter shock on the girl's face, however, and asked, "Why...whatever is the matter, darling?"

"Nothing. He's in the entry. He's brought...a guest. I think I'll go riding." Then quickly crossing the room, she fled through another door, ignoring Lady Thorton's calling after her.

Once outside, she ran toward the stables. Tears of grief flooded her cheeks, and her heart threatened to stop for the pain stabbing at it.

She was relieved to find no one in the stables, and throwing her arms around the neck of her beloved mount, she cried, "Oh, Valerian! I am most certainly not prepared for this!" She took the horse's head in her hands and caressed its velvety nose with her own, allowing rivulets of tears to travel down her face and onto that of the cherished mare. The animal whinnied, understanding her mistress was in distress.

Maria sobbed bitterly. "Valerian! Whatever will I do? I cannot...I cannot watch him love another woman! I shall surely die of it! I believe I will literally die of it, Valerian." She sobbed, wiping her tears on the soft fur of Valerian's face. "How could he?" she continued, feeling as if her breath had been stolen from her somehow. "No forewarning! She simply came walking in like she belonged here. 'You must be little Maria,' she said. Oh, Valerian...she's too beautiful! You should see her. Hair as spun gold and eyes as the finest emeralds. He did not even forewarn me, Valerian. He gave me no indication."

"She's a family acquaintance, Maria."

Maria startled, gasping at the sound of Brock's voice behind her. Tightly clenching her teeth, she did not turn to face him.

"Whatever are you talking about, Brock?" she asked, attempting to sound unflustered.

"Rebecca," came his answer, and the sound of his voice caused excess moisture to flood Maria's mouth. "Her mother and mine are dear old friends," he continued. "She's just come for a brief visit of a few days until her mother arrives for a visit as well. That is all." Maria sensed him take several steps toward her.

"It's fine. You do not have to explain everything to me. She is quite divine, is she not?" Reaching over, she took a comb from its hook on the stable wall and began grooming Valerian's mane. She stiffened, however, when Brock's hand appeared over her shoulder and began stroking Valerian's jaw.

"You've no reason to be angry with me, Maria. It is all quite innocent," he whispered in her ear. Again goose flesh erupted over the entire surface of Maria's body, and she closed her eyes against the euphoria of it.

Quickly turning to face him then, not caring her face was streaked where tears had cascaded, she asked, "You do not understand, Brock! She's a friend of the family is all very well and good. But someday... someday you will...you will..."

"Take vows of marriage?" he finished for her as a frown manifested itself on his brow.

Maria could only nod as she brushed the tears from

31

her blushing cheeks. "You will tell me first, won't you?" she whispered. "You won't simply come back one day with a...with a..."

"Wife?" he finished, still frowning.

She nodded. "Promise me, Brock. Promise me this very minute, Brock Thorton. Promise when the day comes—and I am not ignorant; I know that it must come—yet promise me you will tell me first. Promise you will let me know before you simply arrive one day...with a...with a..."

"Wife."

"Yes. Promise me, Brock. You've no idea how important it is I be given the time to...prepare myself for the...change."

Brock looked down into Maria's tear-filled, pleading eyes. "Maria...I..." He paused, seeming to reconsider what he had meant to say, and then continued, "I promise to you, Maria...that when the time comes for me to announce my engagement, you will be the very first person to know of it." He reached out and brushed a stray strand of hair from her cheek, and Maria thought she might melt at his feet, undone in a puddle of sorrow and joy mingled. "There now," he said, brushing at the strand of hair on her cheek once more. "Do you feel better?"

Maria turned from him and began combing Valerian's mane once more. "I...I suppose," she stammered. Yet the ache in her heart only intensified. In that moment, he had openly admitted he would indeed one day marry. In that moment, it had become a genuinely agonizing reality to Maria.

Taking her shoulders, Brock turned her to face him once more. "Now, come into the house with me," he said, tenderly brushing the tears from her cheeks with the back of one powerful hand.

Maria shook her head, wiping her remaining tears on the sleeve of her dress. "No. No, I am in utter shambles. I look as a child who has only just finished a tantrum."

He chuckled. "Pretty lady, I doubt you have ever borne even the slightest resemblance to a child. Now, come along and see what I've brought you."

"I do not care what you've brought, Brock. I just wanted you home," she admitted to him.

"What an ungrateful thing to say! And after I spent days finding just the right…come along, my pet," he said, taking Maria's arm and linking it with his own.

"It is not another golden-haired woman, is it?" she asked, forcing a smile at last.

Brock chuckled. Removing Maria's arm from his and pulling it around his waist, he held her protectively against him as they walked. "No, Maria. I promise to warn you next time, no matter the circumstance."

Once they had returned to the house, he said, "Now, run upstairs and open that parcel. If you detest it, there isn't much time to replace it. I'll go in to Mother now." He placed an affectionate kiss on her forehead and left.

Maria seemed unable to keep new tears from traveling over her cheeks, for in truth, what comfort was there to be gained from his promise he would tell her when he planned to wed? It was simply further affirmation the nightmare had truly begun. Still, as Maria walked to her chamber, she tried to hope— hope the day would never come when Lord Brockton Thorton would take a wife.

Going to her bed, Maria smiled as she gazed down at the parcel Brock had tossed to her through the open window. She thought of the joy that had washed over her when she first heard Stetson's gallop. She closed her eyes and envisioned Brock astride his mount, smiling up at her the way he had only a short time before. She determined it would be the vision she carried of him—fresh, handsome, and thinking only of her in that moment.

Rather unwillingly, she picked up the parcel and untied the string holding the paper and whatever was within.

Maria gasped at the sight of the gown, its soft, silken folds falling elegantly through the air as she held it up before her. Brock had always brought her a new pair of slippers or boots when he returned home. He insisted she have as many pairs as she could fit in the bottom of her wardrobe. He had always sworn her feet would never be so cold as they were the night he had carried her from her aunt and uncle's loveless cottage. In truth, he would often bring gifts to accompany any new slippers—a dress, a pretty memento. But this dress! Maria could not believe the pure elegance of it. There was no doubt he intended this to be her dress for her coming-out ball. In its white brilliance, it teetered on having the appearance of a wedding dress. And the lace! Never had Maria seen so fine, so delicate, such exquisite lace! Yet there was a sophisticated simplicity about the dress as well.

Carelessly, she dropped the dress she had been wearing to the floor, squealing as she worked at the buttons of the fresh gown. It was a bit more revealing than any frock she had previously worn. Indeed, the bodice of Brock's gifted gown lay ever so slightly off her shoulders. Still, she did not mind. It was beautiful and chosen by Brock's own hand.

She gathered her hair up on the top of her head studying herself in the looking glass. Certainly there was no other way to wear her hair with such a gown and to such an event, and she pinned her raven locks in place. Smiling at her reflection, she turned once more to the package on her bed. Brock had, of course, purchased slippers as well, and they were there within. Maria unwrapped them, marveling at their loveliness. They appeared to be made specifically for the gown, corresponding to it perfectly. As Maria turned the slippers over to examine them further, something caught her eye as it fell from one of the slippers and onto the floor.

A dainty, exquisite string of pearls lay at her feet. She was so astonished at their appearance she paused before picking them up, afraid she had dreamed them, that they might disappear if she attempted to touch them. She gathered her senses quickly enough, however, and picked them up at last. Drawing the precious ornaments to her soft lips, she kissed them and lovingly clutched them to her bosom. Here, indeed, was a treasure from Brock! Not a gown, which would yellow with age, nor slippers, which would wear through. This was something she could always keep near, something to remind her that at one time she had been significant to Lord Brockton Thorton. Such a gift spoke of a deep and abiding affection. Certainly, Maria knew well enough Brock cared for her as his ward, his friend even. He did not care for her as more, certainly not as a lover, though pearls were often the first choice of a gift a man would give to his beloved. Still, Maria chose to fancy it was so, chose to fancy Brock had gifted her a lover's strand of pearls. Each time the lovely pearls caressed the soft skin around her throat, she would pretend it was his intent—to tell her he loved her.

THE *First*

Maria peeked around the corner into the library. There they sat, Lady Thorton, Brock, and the beautiful Rebecca. She winced at the sharp pain in her bosom at the sight of Rebecca but drew strength remembering Brock's assurance to her that Rebecca was merely a friend to the Thorton family.

"Close your eyes," Maria called to the occupants of the library. "I am going to practice my entrance into the ballroom."

"Wonderful, darling!" Lady Thorton called, clapping her hands with excitement. "We are ready. Completely so!"

Carefully, Maria stepped around the corner, fairly floating slowly and elegantly, into the room.

Lady Thorton gasped with delight, and Rebecca looked as if a ghost, rather than a young woman, had just entered the library. Brock was somehow successful at smiling and frowning simultaneously.

Maria could bear it no longer. Abruptly, whirling around and dashing to Lady Thorton, she squealed, "Is it not simply divine? And pearls! Can you imagine it? Pearls, milady! Real pearls!" Maria's smile faded when tears began pouring profusely from the woman's brilliant eyes. "Milady, what ever is the matter? Does the gown not suit? Brock has always been perfect with his selections for me before and—"

"No, no, darling. I love the gown," Lady Thorton sniffled. "It's simply...my little girl...oh, why does time rush by so?" The great beauty leaned forward, planting a kiss on Maria's cheek. "Look at you! Simply look at her, Brock! Hair pulled up...graceful as a butterfly."

"Indeed," Brock muttered, clearing his throat as he rose and went to stand near the fireplace.

"My, my, my, Brock. So this is your Maria. How perfectly that gown fits her. It is amazing...your judging her size so well," Rebecca said. "It is a beautiful gown, Maria. I only hope Mother and I can remain long enough to see you wear it at the ball. But if you will excuse me now, I am rather fatigued and would like to rest." Rebecca stood, haughtily raised her chin, and walked from the room.

"If you will excuse me, as well, darling...I'm in utter distress," Lady Thorton cried, fleeing from the room in tears.

Maria stood, bewildered. "Is...is this a positive response to the gown, Brock? I'm not certain," she asked, unsure as to whether to feel flattered or burst into tears.

"Of course it is," Brock rather grumbled.

"Are you angry with me?" she asked, for he sounded quite agitated. "I know I was so childish out in the stable. But you do forgive me, do you not, Brock?" She could not have him angry with her! She valued his good opinion far too much; it mattered far too much to her.

"Nothing to forgive," he said, seeming to dispel his momentary struggle with gloom. Turning, he smiled and said, "You are going to allow me the first lingering waltz, are you not?"

Maria felt as if an entire flock of doves had taken flight within her bosom. His attention always rendered her breathlessly delighted.

"Oh, yes!" she giggled, too thrilled with his attention and request of a lingering waltz to contemplate heartache for a brief moment. "Shall we practice it now? I'm a bundle of nerves about this whole affair! Please, let's do practice," Maria pleaded.

His smile faded for a moment but returned quickly. "Very well, muffin. We begin thusly. "He took her in his arms, and instantly she felt more alive, joyous, and aflutter.

"Do you know, Brock…you do not seem to tower above me quite as much as you once did. Though I still get an ache in my neck from looking up at you," she giggled.

He smiled, chuckling as they continued to dance. "You flatter the gown," he said.

"It's a beautiful gown. It would look lovely on anyone," she told him, delighted with his compliment.

"Perhaps. Yet on anyone else, the gown would flatter the girl. In this instance, the girl flatters the gown."

"'Tis *you* flatter me so, Brock. But I think it's the dance partner who makes the girl, in this case."

Brock exhaled a heavy sigh as he continued to smile at Maria. "Oh, Maria," he breathed. "Sweet, sweet Maria. Nearly sixteen. It is hard to fathom it. How is it said?" he asked. "'Sweetest at sixteen when never been kissed.' Is that what is said?" His eyes were full of mischief as they always were when he teased her.

"Perhaps it is said as such," Maria said, mischief blooming in her own mind. "Still, however could you be assured it is aptly applied to me, Brock?"

"Assured what is aptly applied to you?" he asked.

"How can you be assured I have never been kissed? For I'll tell you…I have," Maria whispered, as if sharing secrets with a fellow conspirator.

"What?" Brock nearly shouted, instantly ceasing their dance and glaring down at her.

Smiling, she said, "Brock! I do pronounce you are such fun to tease! Look at you, appearing so serious and infuriated."

"You're only teasing me then, Maria?" he asked. All signs of mischief or mirth had abandoned his countenance as he glared at her. Yet Maria smiled, knowing him too well to take his serious expression to heart.

"Maybe," she giggled.

Brock then took her shoulders firmly, his

smoldering, angry eyes burning into her own. "Tell me you are only teasing me, Maria," he growled.

She realized then he was truly unsettled, truly angry. Guilt washed over her, yet she wondered why it should. He wanted no claim to her. Why should he concern himself as to whether she had ever before been kissed?

"Brock, it is not a sin for a young girl to have a kiss stolen before she is sixteen, is it?" she asked him.

Brock rather forcefully released Maria and turned away, his massive chest rising and falling with restrained anger.

Maria walked around to stand before him once more. Taking one of his large, strong hands between her own hands, she said, "Brock, are you truly angry with me? I promise…I was only teasing. Do you think less of me somehow? Please talk to me. This…this has been such a miserable day thus far. I cannot bear to have you angry with me twice in an hour."

She understood then: she was his ward. Her actions reflected upon him, and any bad or improper behavior on her part would find him the bitter bump of gossip.

He closed his eyes for a moment, inhaled deeply once more, and then looked down into her concerned face. Shaking his head, he managed a slight grin as he said, "I am sorry, Maria. It's simply that…you've got to promise me you won't let anyone steal your precious kisses. Ever."

Maria smiled and giggled nervously. "Brock…what do you mean to say? Surely you would not have me an old spinster lady. Someday someone may think enough of me to—"

"Promise me, Maria. No one. Ever." His grin had faded, and he was again sternly glaring down at her.

It was Maria whose anger was kindled then.

"No! I cannot promise you something as ridiculous as what you demand! You will marry. You've told me as much today! I will marry also...and with marriage surely comes a kiss." She was hurt by his hypocrisy for the of sake society's good opinion. In truth, she had no desire for anyone ever to kiss her, save the very man standing before her. As long as she could have Brock's tender kisses on her forehead, she was contented. But the premise was unjust.

Brock appeared greatly unsettled, though his anger seemed to have lessened. He looked away for a moment. His next utterance astounded her as he said, "Then, sweet Maria...I would ask you allow me to kiss you first."

Had she heard him correctly? She was bewildered. Was he, in truth, suggesting he would kiss her? Was he, in truth, implying he wanted to kiss her?

"The...the first?" she stammered. "We...you and I...we kiss one another quite often. Each time you return from an absence, whenever we have had a fun story together, each time you bring me a gift..."

His expression changed again. Maria was astonished as the air of utter confidence and determination he wore almost constantly was lost. "Am I too old then?"

"What?" she asked in a whisper.

"Does it sicken you to think of my kissing you… because I am such a wrinkled-up old gentleman?" He smiled slyly. His demeanor had indeed changed. Maria began to sense a sort of delightful panic rising in her bosom.

"Certainly not," she answered. "I mean to say… what are you talking about, Brock?" She took a step backward, but he caught her hand before she could take another.

"Let us have another practice of the lingering waltz, shall we, Miss Holt." It wasn't a question. He took her in his arms once again and improperly pulled her tightly against his firm body.

Maria was entirely disturbed. They had spent a great amount of time in close contact, even embraced, exchanging affectionate, benign kisses on cheeks and forehead. But somehow this was different—the manner in which he held her, moved with her, most of all the manner in which he was looking at her.

"I make a request of you, sweet Maria," Brock whispered enticingly into her ear. "May I be the first? The first to kiss you…truly kiss you? To savor the sweet confection of your mouth and let you taste the flavor of mine? So that for the rest of your life…if any other man may kiss you, your soul will cry, 'Only Brock. I only wish it were Brock!'"

Maria's eyes widened at the alluring words breathed from his lips. Her mouth ran moist and hot, her skin prickling with goose flesh. She had so often dreamt of such a kiss from Brock, but could it be he truly meant to bless her lips with such a treasure?

Maria shook her head a bit, smiled, and sighed with relief, realizing he was in jest. Entirely in jest.

"That is very arrogant, Brockton Thorton. You talk as if no one could ever compare to you...in...in that respect."

Brock simply said, "Do you doubt it?"

Maria was further assured then of his being only in jest and smiled up into his smoldering eyes. "No, darling Brock. I do not doubt it."

Maria tossed her head back as a giggle rose in her, but the sound was silenced in her throat as she felt Brock's mouth caress the tender flesh of her neck. Instantly straightening, she looked at him in astonishment. The intoxicatingly attractive man grinned. He bent, capturing the string of pearls at her neck with his teeth and tugging at them playfully. When he released the adornment, Maria pushed at his shoulders, stepping away from him.

His smile faded as he at once began to apologize. "Forgive me, Maria. I...was wrong to tease you in such an inappropriate manner."

But Maria had felt the warmth of his lips on her flesh, thrilled at his playful act with the pearls, and she caught his arm to stall him as he turned to leave her.

Though every part of her being trembled with uncertainty, she asked, "Were you, Brock...were you only teasing me?" Hope burned fierce in her heart, desire with even more ferocity.

He paused for a moment, yet not turning to face her. "No," he answered at last.

Maria's heart began to pound with such brutality it pained her. To kiss Brockton Thorton, to feel his lips pressed to hers...it was a dream she dared not wish would come true. But she did wish it.

Swallowing hard and summoning every fragment of courage within her, she asked, "Then...will you? I mean to say...if it would not be an unpleasant task to you...will you indeed?"

Brock turned and looked at her, still frowning. "Will I what, Maria?"

Courage was quickly abandoning her, but she endeavored with what little remained and whispered, "Will you...will you kiss me? I know I am so terribly young in your grown-man's eyes, Brock...and not matured and ravishing as those women you are used to. Still...I..."

Instantly, he gathered her into his powerful arms. A handsome grin of pleasure revealed the dimple in his cheek. Maria's heart was beating so madly she thought she might indeed expire. She fought to slow her quickened breath and hammering heart as Brock kissed her cheek very tenderly, very lingeringly.

"There is nothing on this earth, or in heaven for that matter...nothing I would find more pleasing, my pretty peach," he whispered. Maria sighed, letting her body lean into his. "Still, I forewarn you, Miss Holt...I am about to commence with robbing you of your naiveté," Brock whispered, his mouth so close to her own.

"Well, you had better make haste, milord, before the victim in question is lost in her cowardice," she whispered. In an instant, the perception of his lips pressed to hers drowned her reason.

Brock kissed Maria most sweetly and gently at first, no doubt allowing for her anxious state of mind and inexperience. He paused for a moment, taking her trembling hands and placing them at the back of his own neck. "It is much improved if you...accept and return my affections, Maria."

She glanced away shyly, but he took hold of her chin and directed her face toward his. Finding her mouth once more, he softly caressed her lips with his own, now and again pausing to press a tender kiss to them. Gradually, the kisses he administered to her lengthened, the insistence with which he kissed her increasing until, all at once, he seemed to grow suddenly impatient. Taking her face between his capable hands, Brock's mouth captured hers in a firm and driven kiss. She sensed the moisture of his mouth, felt the moisture of her own increase a hundredfold. As his kiss intensified, Maria felt suddenly freed, liberated, and she commenced in letting her passion for the man she loved break her bonds of hesitation and fear, returning his kisses with vigorous confidence. Brock's need to instruct her ended swiftly as Maria's feelings and instincts escaped the tethers of youth.

As Brock drew Maria into his arms and against

the power of his body, the variation in their ages disappeared. As their mouths mingled in shared affection, she surrendered her soul to him. Everything she felt for him, everything she buried deep within for so long, escaped and was free as he held her there, his hands caressing her soft shoulders, his mouth quenching her thirst for his kiss.

After a time, he broke the seal of their lips, placing a lingering, caressive kiss on her shoulder. He winked at her, smiling as she blushed and glanced away.

"Forgive me, Maria," he whispered, turning her away from him and pulling her back against his torso as his arms tightened about her waist. "But it had to be me. Only me," he said, placing lingering kisses on the back of her neck and then the bareness of her shoulder.

She turned in his arms and looked lovingly into the delicious brown of his eyes. "Yes, Brock," she said, caressing his rugged cheek with one palm. "It could only have been you."

He smiled and playfully tweaked her nose, pulling her hand from his cheek and placing a warm, moist kiss in her palm.

"Was it truly such a terrible day after all?" he asked.

Maria smoothed her hair and, feigning an indifferent manner, said, "No. I suppose not."

"Then off with you, chit," he chuckled. "Compose yourself before dinner, lest my mother suspect me of some tomfoolery where you're about."

Maria smiled at him, her love, her heart's desire.

She paused in leaving him, not wanting to take her gaze from his handsome face.

"Off with you, kitten!" he chuckled. "I have damaged you enough for one day."

Maria nodded, understanding what had happened between them must be kept secret and safe. Further, she understood it was the stuff of dreams, knowing dreams only came true once in a lucky person's lifetime. Still, she tried to reconcile herself to the knowledge of one fleeting moment held in Brock's arms, savoring his delicious kiss. She tried to tell her soul once would be enough. Then she turned from him and hurried up the stairs to her chamber.

$\mathscr{S}$ERENITY

Once isolated within the privacy of her chamber, Maria bolted the door and leaned back against it. Her hands rested at her bosom, her heart thumping wildly to the point of discomfort. Once her breathing had steadied, she could no longer suppress a sigh of delight. Never had she experienced such complete euphoria! She found herself still covered in goose flesh, the sensation of Brock's mouth blissfully lingering on hers. She wished it would never fade. She wished she could spend forever wrapped in his arms, his hot, moist kisses spawning revelry throughout her entire being always.

Quickly, she removed the beautiful gown—Brock's gift to her—and hung it lovingly in the wardrobe. She began to put on the dress she had discarded earlier but then, remembering the lovely Rebecca would be dining in Thorton Manor, chose a dress slightly more mature in cut and line. It was one of Brock's favorites, a peacock blue. He always commented her eyes looked as flashing sapphires whenever she wore it.

Glancing at the clock on her wall, she realized it was already time to go down for dinner. At the thought, her confidence began to teeter. How should she act? Could she meet Brock's gaze without blushing now that they had shared such intimacy?

Her stomach churned nervously as she descended the stairs minutes later.

Lady Thorton and Rebecca were already seated when Maria entered the dining hall.

"Oh! You always look so delightful in that blue, Maria!" Lady Thorton exclaimed as Maria kissed her affectionately on one cheek before taking her seat at the woman's side.

"Thank you, milady. But you flatter me so. Do not forget, I have a looking glass and can see for myself every imperfection. It is pleasing to have your compliments, all the same."

Lady Thorton shook her head and smiled. "You have always been the perfect example of modesty," she sighed. "I fancy you truly see yourself as plain and lacking."

Maria shrugged. "Good evening, Rebecca," Maria said, smiling across the table at the beauty sitting there.

"And to you, Maria," Rebecca said.

"Wherever is Brock?" Lady Thorton wondered aloud.

Maria smiled. Lady Thorton always insisted on promptness at the dinner hour.

"You're too impatient, Mother," Brockton said, entering and taking his seat at the head of the table. "I had to post several important letters. They couldn't wait, I'm afraid," he apologized to his mother, smiling conspiratorially at Maria.

She felt herself begin to blush and quickly looked away, the blissful residual sensation of his touch causing her to break into goose flesh.

The meal was served, and all in the Thorton Manor dining hall began eating as they enjoyed light, yet pleasant conversation. Maria avoided looking at Brock often, however. She began to feel overly warm each time she did glance at him. He was forever grinning at her in a manner hinting at his possessing some secret knowledge shared by only one other person in the room—that person being herself, of course.

After a time, at the memory of being wrapped in the power of Brock's arms and when her lips began to tingle at the thought of his remembered kiss, Maria began fanning herself with one hand.

"Are you too warm, darling?" Lady Thorton asked.

Maria abruptly stopped the motion and answered, "Um…yes. Just a bit." She glanced to the head of the table to find Brock smiling with eyebrows raised in an amused expression.

"Really, darling?" Lady Thorton continued. "I thought it was a bit chilly in here myself. Are you feeling quite all right?"

"Oh, I think Maria feels wonderful, Mother," Brock answered, chuckling.

Maria stared at him in amazement, her eyes widening in disbelief. Apparently, and blessedly, the other two persons at the dining table had not understood the underlying meaning of his lordship's remark. Maria was grateful. He winked playfully at her, however, and she was undone again, rapidly fanning herself with one hand.

"Well, I hope so," Lady Thorton remarked. Then to Rebecca, "When will your dear mother be arriving, Rebecca?"

"The day after next I'm hoping, milady. I am so very anxious to see her," Rebecca answered.

Maria looked up nervously at Brock again only to find him still grinning mischievously at her.

Stop! she mouthed silently to him.

What? he silently mouthed in response, feigning ignorance. Maria gasped slightly as she watched Brock, then looking intently at her mouth, slowly moisten his lips with his tongue. It was a purely scandalous insinuation!

"Are we missing something, children?" Lady Thorton asked, looking from Maria to her son and then back again.

Maria dropped her gaze to her plate as she felt the crimson of a heated blush rising to her cheeks once more.

"Why, darling…you do look a bit overheated. Do not you think so, Brock?" Lady Thorton asked, concerned.

Brock looked down at his plate and answered, "Yes, I find her very warm."

Maria gasped again, unable to fathom his outrageous comment and causing herself to choke on a bit of her food.

"My goodness!" Lady Thorton exclaimed. "I do believe you're unwell, Maria."

Brock chuckled lowly.

"There is nothing whatsoever amusing about this, Brockton! I tell you, Rebecca...I find it very hard to believe he is a grown man at times." Lady Thorton sighed, patting Maria helpfully on the back.

"I am well. In truth, milady. I am well," Maria choked, swallowing hard and clearing her throat. "Truly."

Lady Thorton frowned. "Very well. Are you certain?"

"I think—"Brock began.

"Yes. I'm certain," Maria interrupted, scowling severely at him.

Lady Thorton looked from her son to Maria and back to her son again. A knowing smile crossed her features. "Very well. Let us finish our meal. I am certain Rebecca thinks us most uncivilized if our behavior at the dinner hour is any indication."

"Oh, I assure you, not at all, milady." Looking to Maria, she added, "Mother and Lady Thorton were schoolgirls together, you know."

❧

Following dinner, Jacob Peterson arrived. He and

Brock disappeared together. Lady Thorton retired early, leaving Maria and Rebecca alone together in the library. This was not Maria's ideal of a pleasing after-dining activity, but there seemed little else to do but endure.

"Brock and I were playmates as children," Rebecca continued. "We were very close then. Oh, the hours we used to spend riding together and playing mischief on our parents. I cannot believe it has been so long ago. He was handsome even as a boy. One could tell for certain, even then, he would be what he is now."

Maria fidgeted uncomfortably. Something in the back of her mind was telling her that perhaps Rebecca's visit was not as insignificant as it appeared to be.

"I've only been here for three years," Maria said. "The family has been so wonderful to me."

"Yes. They seem quite fond of you. And now...now you're to have your coming-out! I'm sure you will have suitors lined up for miles outside Brock's door!"

"I hope not," Maria mumbled to herself.

"Oh, you mustn't be nervous about them. It is ever so amusing to have all the young men vying for your attention!"

There was only one man on earth whose attention Maria longed for. She smiled to herself, thinking on their moments together previously that afternoon.

"See there...it does sound fun. Does it not?" Rebecca said, mistakenly reading Maria's thoughts.

"This is far past the proper bedtime for little girls,

ladies," Brock's voice boomed suddenly from the doorway.

Rebecca rose and, smiling, said, "I am a bit done in. Do you mind if I retire, Maria? It was a long piece to travel today."

Maria rose as well and answered, "Of course, of course. I'm feeling fatigued myself. We can talk tomorrow."

As Rebecca floated out of the room, she paused, kissing Brock sweetly on one cheek. "Good night, Brock dearest," she said, smiling rather beguilingly up at him.

"Good night," he called as she climbed the stairs.

Maria was hot with irritation. She did not like Rebecca's infatuation with Brock, which was becoming more and more obvious.

"Will you retire as well then, Maria?" Brock asked, striding toward her.

"Yes. And by the way…your behavior was abominable at dinner, Brockton Thorton!" she scolded him in a whisper.

"Oh. Is that all? I was afraid you were going to scold me for my behavior in the library this afternoon," he teased, lowering his voice.

Maria smiled and blushed. "I would never scold you for that," she whispered. "Still, I could not believe you at dinner, Brock! How old do you claim to be anyway?" she teasingly reprimanded, moving to walk past him.

He chuckled and caught her arm. "Do you favor the gown?"

"I've told you...I adore the gown! Now, let's retire. I am ever so fatigued."

"Yes. Let's," he whispered, linking her arm through his own and escorting her toward the stairs.

"What do you want for your birthday, pretty lady?" he asked suddenly as they began climbing the staircase together. His touch, however simple, was the touch of heaven to her, and she caressed his forearm where her hand lay in escort.

"You've given me your gift already," she said, smiling at him.

"How kind, Maria! To refer to the affair in the library this afternoon as my gift to you," he whispered, smiling.

"Would you please stop? You are intolerable! I meant the dress, of course. And the slippers and...and the lovely string of pearls, Brock!" she sighed, pausing at the top of the stairs as she gazed lovingly up at him. "I could not have imagined such gifts...not in the world! Thank you so much, Brock...for all your beautiful and treasured gifts to me."

"Oh, those," he said, smiling. "You are welcome for them, naturally, pretty pet. But they were not for your birthday. Now, what do you really desire?"

The thought crossed her mind that her utmost desire would be to relive with him those precious moments in the library. However, she answered, "Oh...I cannot imagine. I have everything! What could I possibly be in need of?"

"Well, I must purchase something for you. After all, you will only be sixteen once, now won't you? Let me think…what would you ask for? Jewels? That is really the only thing women like to receive, is it not?"

Maria exhaled dramatically. "Stop. Just stay as long as you can this time. That would be the greatest gift you could offer me."

He smiled. "Very well. I will try. Shall we take Rebecca riding tomorrow? I do not think I can stand to lie around too long."

They had reached the door leading to Maria's chamber. "Yes. Valerian so misses Stetson when you are away. Perhaps Bay Muffin would do for Rebecca. She's very calm."

He smiled and nodded in agreement. "Sleep well then," he said.

"I will. Good night." She stood on the tips of her toes and made to kiss his cheek as she had done for so many years.

Brock shook his head at her. "No, no, Maria. Those days are behind us. You have sampled my mouth now. Can you stand on the pretense you honestly prefer my cheek?"

"What?" Maria exclaimed in a whisper, looking about quickly to ensure their solitude. "What a lecherous thing to say! Do you mean to imply that I—"

She was silenced then as his mouth seized her own and proceeded to prove itself far more coveted, indeed, than his cheek. He ended the kiss all too quickly and held her lovely face in his hands, smiling triumphantly down at her.

"You are a beauty, my pet," he whispered. "And utterly addictive." He crossed the corridor to his own chamber, turning to look at her once more. "Sweet dreams, pretty peach," he said with a wink before disappearing into the darkness of his own chamber.

ℛEVELATION

As the weeks passed, it was still apparent Rebecca was in love with Brock. However, Maria found she had misjudged the fair woman. Rebecca proved to be a very pleasant companion, and Maria could not condemn her for falling victim to the same fate as she, loving Brockton Thorton. Brock paid Rebecca little heed, and Maria soon fell into an easy sense of comfort in the girl's company. She did not feel threatened by her existence or presence at Thorton Manor any longer.

Rebecca's mother arrived, and she and Lady Thorton spent hours each day in the parlor, giggling as giddy schoolgirls. Maria thought it very reassuring to learn women could retain something of their youthful sensibilities. She found she enjoyed Rebecca's company as well. They had become friends, if only in slim means.

Brock continued to taunt Maria. His manner was distinctly different than it had been in the past. Though every ounce of reason and common sense told her she must be mistaken, it seemed his endless teasing had given way to pure flirtation. Much to her disappointment, however, day after day began and ended without his ever intimating he would again kiss her as he had that first day of his return.

Slowly, Maria attempted to step back into a routine. Business matters took a great deal of Brock's time, but when he could spare a moment, they went riding or talked or went for walks, as they always had. Much of Maria's day, however, was spent helping Lady Thorton and Rebecca's mother, Lady Dellancy, in the preparations for Maria's coming-out. The impending event consumed so much time she had begun to dread it. She had no desire to make a spectacle of herself or to have swarms of thin, whiskerless young men attempting to receive permission to pay court to her. She only wished it were over and done with or, better yet, that it had never been conceived at all.

On the morning of her sixteenth birthday, Maria rose before the sun, restless and awash with anxiety. There was an odd, nervous anticipation nagging in the back of her mind, and she sensed it had nothing to do with her coming-out, which was to take place the next day.

As was her habit when feeling unsettled and Brock was occupied with duties and business, Maria found herself in the stables grooming Valerian. The horse seemed pleased to have her there. Or perhaps it was the long brushing the mare received whenever her mistress was agitated that pleased the animal.

"Oh, my sweet Valerian. I feel so oddly anxious. As if...it's so hard to explain. Even to you. I feel as if something...something...very...significant is awaiting at the bend."

Maria continued to brush the mare for several minutes. The sun was just rising, and dawn was still crisp, cool, and invigorating. She drew in a deep breath of morning air and reveled in the refreshment it brought to her body. Suddenly, she felt her senses prickling, and a moment later Brock spoke from behind her.

"You're up early," he said.

She turned to see him standing just inside the stables studying her with a strange, worried sort of expression.

"Yes. It is such a beautiful morning, and I could not sleep it away," she answered, smiling at him.

He quickly strode to her, taking hold of her shoulders. Frowning as he searched her face, he asked, "You do...you do care for me...do you not, Maria?"

It seemed a ridiculous question. Of course he knew she cared for him. Though she tried not to nest on the thought, she feared he suspected how deeply she cared for him as well. Her unsettled senses were quieted quickly, however, when she then realized he was, as always, in jest.

"Of course!" she told him. "That is the silliest question you've ever asked me, Brock. And well you know it." She giggled and turned her attention to Valerian again. "I'll not tumble to your silly bait for a compliment."

Yet the prickling sensation at the back of her neck had not subsided and, in fact, intensified when he spoke again.

"You're sixteen today," he stated as if it were as yet unknown to anyone in the world.

"Profound, Brock. Very profound," Maria giggled. Yet her nervousness lingered.

Suddenly, he took hold of her shoulders once more and spun her to face him. She stared at him in awe, for never had she seen such an expression of determination on his face. At least not since the night he had come and taken her away from her uncle's home years before.

"I need to know, Maria…before Peterson arrives this afternoon. You…you do care for me?"

She paused in answering, stunned again by the seemingly ridiculous question. "Of course, Brock. How can you even stand before me and doubt it?"

He released his hold on her shoulders and ran one hand through his hair in a gesture of frustration. "No, no, no. I know you feel indebted to me, to all of us… for taking you from those people. That is not what I mean to ask you. I'm asking…I mean to say, you do care for me…not just a feeling of…obligation toward me?"

Maria turned away, unable to face him as understanding began to wash over her. He was trying to draw her out, to coax her into openly admitting her love, her passion for him.

"You know I care for you," she admitted. "And even though you are going through this ridiculous charade of asking…I…I have no doubt you at least suspect how tremendous my caring is for you."

She heard him exhale a heavy sigh, as if he had been holding his breath. "I've something for you, Maria," he said then. "I hope you do not think it vain or shallow of me to give this to you."

She turned to see he held a small box in one hand. He held it out toward her in a gesture that she should take it from him. He looked so profoundly anxious, so thoroughly worried, and it concerned her. She smiled at him and took the box form his hand.

"May I open it now? Or must I wait until breakfast?" she asked, curious at what lay within. What could he be afraid to give her?

Brock smiled, and the sight of his boyish dimple sent her stomach tumbling with delight. "You must open it now, of course," he said. "Do you think I've come out here before the sun in order that you might wait until breakfast, chit?"

Maria giggled as she opened the tiny box. Inside, on a bed of red velvet, lay an exquisitely crafted locket—a lovely golden oval locket, hanging from a dainty gold chain.

"Oh, Brock!" Maria breathed. "How…how exquisite!" She was truly enchanted. The locket was ornate with delicate engravings of a floral nature on the face. It was beautiful! Maria held it up to better see it in the morning sunlight, and as she did she noticed an engraving on the locket's backside.

"*Maria, Born For My Sake*," she whispered as she

read the engraving on the locket. "*Forever Yours, Brock.*"

Tears filled Maria's eyes as her fingertips gently caressed the beloved words engraved in gold. "Thank you," she whispered, continuing to gaze down at the locket, not wanting to look up and reveal the tears in her eyes.

"Are not you anxious to open it?" Brock asked unexpectedly.

"Open it?" Maria whispered to herself as she used her thumbnail to test the tiny latch. As the locket opened, Maria could not believe what rested within. A small likeness of him…of Brock! It was somewhat brownish, not a color painting as the miniatures she'd seen before. This was him! An actual likeness of his face!

"It's new. It's called a daguerreotype or some such word. Remarkable, is it not? They actually capture your very image somehow."

"It's you," Maria whispered.

"Well, of course it's me! Who do you think I would put in a locket I intended to give to you? Do you like it, or don't you?"

"It is…your very image," she whispered in dismay again as she let a finger carefully touch the small likeness.

"Maria!" Brock sighed with exasperation. His frown softened, however, when she looked up, and he saw tears streaming over her cheeks.

"Oh, Brock!" Maria could only whisper as she threw her arms around his neck.

"It pleases you then?" he asked tenderly.

She was silent, clinging to him as tears rolled freely down her face. A kind of frenzied panic was fighting to seize control of her. The knowledge of something about to happen was upon her again. She tightened her embrace and buried her face in his shoulder. Never! Never would she let him go again! He was hers. Somehow, he must be. He must belong to her! To be hers alone, and she his.

"You're going to leave, aren't you?" she sobbed.

Brock's arms suddenly tightened about her small form, pulling her snuggly against him. "Yes," he admitted. "But I always come back, don't I?"

"It's different this time. There's something you're not telling me, Brock." Maria looked up into the worried countenance of his face, pleading an answer. "Please, Brock. I can sense it."

Brock forced a smile and wiped a tear from her cheek with the back of his hand. "You're just overly anxious about the gala event tomorrow. That's it, is it not?"

She was angry. She pushed at him hard enough so he was caught off guard, stumbling backward and into a pile of straw, landing hard on his backside.

Maria gasped as his eyes closed, his body having gone limp and unmoving.

"Brock! Brock! I'm so sorry! It's simply that…" She ran to him, kneeling beside him. Still he did not move. "Brock, please!" she cried.

Then his eyes opened, and he grinned mischievously.

"Maria! Such violence in a young woman. And on the eve of her coming-out, to boot!"

Maria hit him hard in the stomach. "It was not amusing, Brock! I was truly concerned for your well-being!"

He lingered in the hay, chuckling to himself for a moment. When he sat up, resting on one elbow, he smiled at her. But Maria's frustration caused her anger to ignite once again.

"Can you never be serious?" she cried, pushing at him repeatedly.

"Maria."

"I mean it. I'm very upset, and there you sit, playing cruel pranks!" She stood and kicked at his legs with one foot.

He chuckled and caught her ankle in his grip. "Maria. Settle yourself. I was only taunting you," he said, smiling as she struggled to free her ankle. "Did I give you these boots? They do not look at all familiar." He chuckled, studying the foot he held firmly in hand.

Completely exasperated, Maria resigned herself to sitting down beside him. "No, Brock. Your mother and I bought these together." It was no use. He was obviously avoiding telling her what she felt he knew.

"Give me the trifle," he said. Without sitting up, she held her hand open toward him.

He took the locket, and she lifted her hair so he could fasten the chain's clasp at the back of her neck. Then she rested her head on the stable floor and lifted the locket, opening it to study the likeness within.

"Mother would up and entirely expire if she were to witness this," he muttered under his breath.

"What?" Maria asked, not heeding his remark, so mesmerized was she by the miracle of his likeness in her hand.

"Properly brought-up ladies and gentlemen do not romp about in the stable straw, Maria," Brock said, standing up and brushing himself off. He offered his hand to her, and she accepted, letting him pull her to her feet. "Happy birthday," he said, grinning as he made ready to leave.

"Brock," Maria began softly, "I cannot express to you how…what a perfect gift this is for you to gift me."

"Well, it is your sixteenth. I wanted you to have at least one pleasant memory of it." He smiled down at her, and she fancied he was wistful. The expression of profound uncertainty again crossed his features.

"Sweetest at sixteen when—"he mumbled.

"I know. I know," she interrupted, clamping one hand over his mouth. "When will you ever quit teasing me about it?" She removed her hand immediately from his mouth when she felt the moistness of his tongue against her palm. The gesture rendered her light-headed.

Brock chuckled. "That is not what I was going to say. But now that you've brought the fact to light again…yes, you have already been kissed…and by me." He smiled at her and added, "It was perfect, was it not?"

Maria felt indignant. "Was it? I do not clearly remember. It must have been very common, or I would certainly remember it more distinctly." She curtsied mockingly and took several steps toward the stable doors to leave.

"Common?" he exclaimed, catching her arm. "Maria, there is nothing common about me."

She raised her eyebrows. "Really? Do not you find that a rather smug opinion of yourself—"

She was in his arms at once. "If you want me to kiss you again, Maria…all you have to do is request it of me," he whispered.

She watched Brock's enticing mouth as he spoke. The roguish grin he wore sent her heart to hammering.

"I did not say I…" she began, but as his lips brushed hers lightly, the words caught in her throat. He drew away a little and grinned again. The emotions being restrained within caused her to tremble in his embrace.

"Please, do not tease me, Brock. You do not understand," she pleaded.

He was serious then and whispered, "Very well. I will not tease." And his mouth seized her own, raining exhilaration on every shred in her body. Heated, moist, and driven, his kiss ravaged her sanity it seemed. She wanted nothing but to taste his mouth mingled with her own.

For an instant, her mind pictured him as the towering lord's son who had rescued her. It was simply inconceivable she was now in his arms receiving the blissful rain of his impassioned affections. Oh, how she did love him! How she basked in the feel of his touch and taste of his kisses!

She wondered if he still perceived her as the small, neglected child he had found so long ago. Surely not. And when he broke from her and their eyes met, she was certain he had taken notice of her having grown up.

"Now," he said, pressing his mouth to hers one last time, "off to breakfast or Mother will think I'm corrupting her little darling." Taking her hand, he led her to the house in silence as she followed, Maria wondering all the time if her weakened knees could continue to carry her.

※

Shortly after midday meal, Brock entered the parlor, gravely somber. His lordship had entered the parlor, and Maria desperately missed the lighthearted man who had played at seducing her in the stables earlier that morning. Rebecca, her mother, and Lady Thorton looked up as he entered as well. Brock glanced to Maria, and she fancied the color had completely abandoned his face.

Turning his attention to his mother, he said, "Jacob Peterson has arrived and is awaiting us in my study."

The smile faded from Lady Thorton's face. She reached over, taking Maria's hand firmly in her own. "Come along, darling," was all she said.

"Excuse us for a time, will you, ladies?" Lady Thorton said as she left Rebecca and her mother in the parlor.

The prickle returned once more to Maria's neck. She stood and followed Brock and his mother across the entryway and into the study that had once belonged to Lord Richard Thorton and now held the secrets of his son, Lord Brockton Thorton.

As they entered the room, Jacob Peterson cleared his throat and returned his spectacles to the bridge of his nose, having finished their polishing.

"Let us all sit," he said, motioning to the chairs situated before Brock's writing table.

Maria and Lady Thorton obeyed, but Maria watched as Brock strode to the window behind his writing table and stood as a tree, tall, unmoving, and stiff. "Get on with the task, Jacob," he growled, folding his powerful arms across his broad chest.

"Well, yes…of course. Well, then…Miss Holt… this concerns instructions given in your father's will," Jacob began.

Maria nodded. Lady Thorton fidgeted with a handkerchief in her lap.

"Yes. Well," Jacob continued. "You see…as you well know, your father and the late Lord Thorton, being such close friends as they were…well…perhaps it would be best if I simply read the information directly from the will."

"Perhaps," Brock grumbled.

Jacob nervously cleared his throat and read, "'… feel it would be in the best interest of my daughter that, at the age of eighteen, she be wed to Brockton Richard Thorton, son of Richard Benton Thorton. It is my wish that at the age of sixteen she be told of her betrothal, thus allowing her sufficient time to accept this arrangement.

In my personal documents, I have included a letter to my daughter, Maria, further explaining the reasons for my agreeing to her betrothal to the younger Thorton when she was but three years of age.'"

Jacob paused and handed a sealed envelope to Maria. He then said, "Miss Holt, I leave you now to consider this revelation." He looked back at Brock, who still stood stiffly before the window.

"I'll leave you as well," Lady Thorton said, standing and quickly exiting behind Jacob. Maria looked to Brock. He stood unmoving and silent.

Her body trembled. She found breath elusive for a moment as she carefully opened the letter from her father. There she read:

My darling Maria,

You have no doubt been told of your betrothal to young Thorton. I am sure it will come as quite an astonishing revelation to you, but I pray read on.

Richard Thorton and I have been closer than brothers. When you were but three years of age, he and his family arrived for a visit. With him he brought young Brockton. I was immediately impressed by him, though he was no more than nine years of age at the time.

Richard and I discussed our concern for our children. We wanted security, happiness, and love for them both. The idea was conceived by your loving mother, who saw in Brockton all the things she would wish for you to have in a companion.

As we four parents watched the two of you together, we

*came to the conclusion it would be a magnificent match...
security for you both and, no doubt, a loving relationship,
in time.*

*I would ask that you trust me and fulfill this obligation.
You will not regret it. It is best, and I will die with peace of
mind knowing you will not go against my wishes.*

Your loving father,
Charles Holt

Maria set the letter aside and looked to Brock. He
stood still unmoving. She must be dreaming! To wed
Brock? To be his wife? Surely he had not agreed to this!
Was this a new revelation to him as well?

"Have you known?" Maria asked uncertainly.

"Yes," he said.

"And...you never told me?"

"No."

"Why ever not, Brock? Why did you not tell me?"
she asked, rising from her chair and taking several steps
toward him.

"I could not. I was bound by my own father and
yours," he said. She could sense no emotion in his voice.

"All this time, you've known. All this time," she
whispered.

"Yes."

"Did...did you agree to this?" she asked hesitantly,
fearing the pain his answer might bring.

"Yes. When I was twelve."

"Twelve? That is hardly old enough to...is it
agreeable with you now, Lord Thorton?" she questioned

as an overwhelming sense of dread began to rise in her being at anticipation of his answer.

"Yes." Still he showed no emotion either through his expression or intonation of voice.

"Everything…the relationship we have come to share…everything as of recent…were you only trying to convince yourself this would be a tolerable situation? Or were you in earnest?"

He was silent.

"Brock?" she pleaded.

He drew in a heavy breath and muttered, "You are asking me to confess things I have guarded for years."

Maria rallied her courage. She could not fathom where within her it came from, but it surfaced then. "There is nothing…nothing I have dreamed of more than our belonging to each other, Brock. I have loved you since the first moment I saw you through the door of that miserable cottage. But…I could not be happy unless you…unless you actually want this too. I mean, I must appear as a child to you! If you are simply fulfilling an obligation…" She stopped when she heard her own words. In the stable! What was it he had asked her only that morning? He had asked her if she cared for him. Not only held an obligation to him. Maria was filled with a sudden, boundless elation and went to stand directly before him.

"You are young, Maria. You see me as the knight in shining armor who rescued you when you were but thirteen. That is not love," he said flatly.

"No. Not the sort a married couple should share,

perhaps. But I do love you, Brock. More than just a maiden would love her rescuer. I live for you to come home and be here with me! I dream of being in your arms every moment, of touching your face, of your kisses." He looked down at her, and she continued, "I know I am terribly young at this moment in your eyes. But I will grow older. I know I can make you love me, Brock. Only give me the opportunity to prove it to you."

"You do babble on at times," Brock said, a smile breaking across his face. "You've loved me, have you? Since the very moment you saw me at your uncle's house through that door, is it? Well, I will tell you something. You were three the first time I saw you. I despised females, as a rule. They were all fragile, vain, and shy. And not a one could sail a decent toy boat across our lake."

He smiled and brushed a strand of hair from Maria's face. She trembled at the simple touch as he continued, "I was an experienced man of nine then, you understand. Our family visited yours once. I reluctantly entered your father's house, and there you sat. Long black ringlets, an immense blue ribbon around your head, lace cascading everywhere. I sighed, thinking you would be an intolerable brat. Then I sat when your mother offered me a chair. You stood up suddenly and ran to me, much like you do now when I arrive home after a long absence." Maria felt tears fill her eyes as his voice broke when speaking of her greeting him after his absences. "You climbed up into my lap and threw your arms around my neck. I tried to push you away, but you held fast to my shoulders. I remember you kept sticking your finger in this infernal dimple on my cheek and giggling. You turned to your mother and said, 'He's very handsome, Mother. Do you think he would kiss me if I asked him?'"

Maria gasped and put a hand to her mouth. He had kissed her when she asked him to. It was nearly prophetic. She brushed a tear from her cheek as he continued once more, "Your mother was mortified, naturally. But I…I was enchanted." He reached out, taking her hand in his and raising it to his lips briefly.

"And then, when the adults had returned to their own conversation, you took my face between your tiny, soft hands, smiled up at me, and kissed me exactly on the mouth."

"Oh, no! Tell me I did not!" Maria asked, somewhat humiliated.

Brock chuckled. "Yes, you did. It was as pure honey to me. We spent the rest of the visit together, you and I. We went for walks, invented games to play, and when it was time for my family to leave, I took you aside for a moment and whispered in your ear, 'Will you marry me when we grow up, pretty little girl?' You nodded vigorously and kissed me exactly on the mouth once more. I've had to wait thirteen long years to taste the honey of your kisses again."

Maria let go of the shyness that had previously kept her from entirely reveling in the intimate moments shared with Brock. Reaching up, she entangled her fingers through his thick, beautiful hair.

"I knew it would feel just as this," she whispered. "I've wanted to do this for as long as I can remember," she said, smiling up at him. Then she raised herself on her toes, kissing him softly on the chin.

"Regaining the confidence found only in toddlers, are you?" Brock whispered as he gazed at her mouth, moistening his own lips.

Maria nodded and pulled his head to her own, kissing him exactly on the mouth. As she moved to release him, he pulled her tightly against his perfect form, kissing her ferociously, wantonly, and without reprieve. Maria was lost, once again, in the passion ablaze between them—lost in love and desire and dreams that would be realized. She would own Brockton! She would own him—his heart, his mind, his passion—and he would own her. In two years he would take complete possession of her, and in that instant she knew...she was born to be Lord Brockton Thorton's wife!

AWAY

The next day was nothing but bedlam! Lady Thorton was so determined the coming-out should be entirely sophisticated and perfect, she kept everyone occupied the entire day. Each member of the household hopped from one thing to the next, hardly having a moment to catch a breath.

Compared with the revelation she was to marry Brock, to Maria the coming-out seemed like one single droplet in a rain barrel. She awoke that morning certain she had dreamt the assembly with Jacob Peterson regarding her father's will. She was even more certain she had dreamt the conversation between Brock and herself in the study afterward.

It was inconceivable he could love her—actually be in love with her! After all, she was merely sixteen, he a completely grown man of twenty-two. Surely she had dreamt it. But that afternoon when Lady Thorton asked to see her in the library, Maria knew it was, in fact, certainty. She, Maria Castillo Holt, was the betrothed of the obsessively coveted Lord Brockton Thorton!

"I've already spoken with Brock, Maria," Lady Thorton began as she closed the library door, ensuring their privacy. "As Brock explained, your engagement will not be announced for one year. We have all agreed then will be the appropriate time for it. Therefore, considering the fact this arrangement is, to say the least, more than agreeable to the both of you...well, to simply come out and say it, darling, it would be... safer...more proper...if Brock were to live away from the house for a time."

Maria instantly became ill. "But, milady...why? I have lived here for three years! Surely it was proper before. I do not see why—"

Lady Thorton inhaled deeply, fanning herself nervously. "It is not so much the issue of propriety that concerns me, darling. More so...the feelings you and Brock share for one another. It would be too strenuous...too difficult to...well, certainly too tempting for Brock. Perhaps not for you...your being a woman and very young. But for him...his age...and his knowing now how strong your feelings are for him."

Understanding enlightened Maria's mind. "Oh. I see," she said, dropping her eyes to the floor. In her inexperience, Maria had not previously thought that perhaps the strain of being in love yet having to wait two years to marry might become taxing for her and Brock.

Then Lady Thorton continued. "Oh! I'm so very

relieved, my dear…that you understand what I'm trying to convey to you! I was afraid I was going to have to give a lecture on the weaknesses of men when it comes to controlling their physical desires for a woman."

Lady Thorton's relief obviously turned immediately to nervousness once again when she saw Maria's eyes widen in sudden, complete comprehension.

Maria laughed nervously. "Oh, milady! I am certain you have nothing to fear along such venues where Brock is concerned. He is the epitome of the perfect gentleman!"

Lady Thorton smiled and quirked one disbelieving brow. "He is that. At least under normal circumstances. But where you are concerned, darling…well, it is best, Maria. In fact, it was Brock who suggested it. After all, who better to judge his strengths and weaknesses where his lover is concerned than the man himself? He plans to leave on the morrow."

"On the morrow?" Maria cried, jumping to her feet. "But he only just arrived! He has only been here a short time!"

"Yes, I know, darling. But he confided in me you have become much too tempting for him not to…as he put it…keep his good sense about him where you are concerned."

Maria nodded. Suddenly she understood perhaps more than she thought herself capable. She knew where she wanted to be every moment of the day: entangled in his arms. Two years was a very long time to elude the necessity of being there.

Lady Thorton gathered the girl into her motherly embrace. "Just think, my sweet…in two years' time you really will be mine. At long last."

Maria looked up into the woman's beautifully matured face. "I am yours now, milady. You well know you are both mother and friend to me." She smiled and lovingly embraced the woman once more. "Now, I must be off. I suppose I should look the best I am capable this evening. There is so much yet to do." With a quick kiss to one cheek of Lady Thorton, she took her leave.

Maria spent, at the least, an hour crying into her pillows once barricaded in her chambers. How could she live without the prospect of Brock coming home every few months? Surely he would visit! Surely he would not stay away the entire two years! And why had her father insisted they wait until she was eighteen to marry? Many young women were married at sixteen, and many who were did not even wish to marry the men they were forced to wed. Why could not Maria marry Brock at once? Why had her father stipulated the two years? She could not live a year without him near! Yet she must. She wiped her tears, realizing then whether two days or two years, she would wait to belong to Brock, for belonging to him would be worth the torture of missing him. As long as she would spend eternity in his arms afterward, she could wait a year to feel his lips pressed to hers once more, his strong arms about her.

❧

"Maria? Darling? May I come in?" Lady Thorton asked from beyond the closed door of Maria's chambers. "It is nearly time. The guests have assembled in the ballroom."

Maria studied herself in the looking glass. "Yes, come in," she answered finally.

Lady Thorton caught her breath at the sight of the lovely creature her eyes beheld upon entering the room. "Darling! You...you look...exquisite!"

Maria felt sickened with anxiety. "Hardly exquisite, milady. Perhaps dowdy, plain, ordinary—homely even—but not exquisite. I cannot possibly go down with all those people looking on! And besides, what point is there? I have no interest in being courted by anyone but your son," she said, curling a long raven ringlet around her finger.

"Oh, darling! You are such a modest young lady. That is quite refreshing. Now, Brock is waiting just downstairs to escort you in. He will have the first dance as well. Just remember, you are more beautiful than anything those assembled in the ballroom have ever seen! I assure you of that. And Brock loves you. Nothing else matters." Lady Thorton kissed Maria's cheek encouragingly and opened the door. "Now, do not twist your pearls so, dear. They will break apart."

"Oh! You see, milady...I was not even aware that I was fidgeting. I am so anxious!" Maria whispered as they descended the stairs together. She had wanted to wear the locket Brock gave her, but the pearls looked so beautiful with the dress, she relented and wore them. As she and Lady Thorton proceeded down the stairs, she tried not to twist the dainty adornment.

As Maria reached the bottom of the staircase, Brock turned, smiling dashingly at her. Involuntarily, she broke into goose flesh as she remembered the moment in the library when he had taken the string of pearls in his teeth before he kissed her. Subconsciously, for the memory purely delighted her, Maria's fingers toyed with the tiny orbs once more.

"Maria," Brock greeted her. He bent, placing a lingering kiss on her bare shoulder.

"Brockton!" Lady Thorton scolded in a whisper, looking about quickly to be certain no one had witnessed her son's indecent and brazen act.

"Now, now, Mother. Do not pull the reins too tight or the leather will snap," he whispered, winking at Maria.

Warm security flooded through Maria's entire being as Brock took her hand and placed it ceremoniously in the crook of his arm. She marveled at how naturally her own arm fit with his.

"Now, you just remember, pretty kitten," he whispered to her, "you belong to me. This is purely performance. Understood?"

Maria giggled as they approached the ballroom. "Of course. I never wanted to go through with this anyway, remember?"

A moment before the doors to the ballroom swung

open, Brock bent and quickly kissed Maria's shoulder once more.

"Brockton!" his mother scolded as the doors opened wide and Maria stood radiant and blushing on Brock's arm for all those assembled to behold.

There went up a great noise of cheering and awed responses, and Maria curtsied gracefully before Brock led her to the ballroom floor. Once in the center of the room, a loud voice boomed, "Lord Brockton Richard Thorton and Miss Maria Castillo Holt."

Again cheering went up as the musicians began to orchestrate the lingering waltz. Brock smiled down at Maria, and the light in his eyes made her feel perfectly lovely! Her hair was piled high with a strand here and there hanging freely, each in a perfect ringlet. Her skin was soft and fragrant, and she moved with the grace of some fabled fairy. In his arms, she felt beautiful.

As Maria gazed up into Brock's captivating expression, she realized for herself why it was necessary for them to be apart. The longing to reach up and run her fingers through his chestnut-gold mane was nearly impossible to deny.

"There are confessions in my mind, my pet," he whispered to her as they danced. "Certain things I wish to tell you…but now is not the time."

"Tell me," she demanded, smiling at him.

"I cannot," he said, smiling. "And I must leave you after this dance."

Her smile faded. "Cannot you be somewhat attentive?" she pleaded.

Brock simultaneously smiled and frowned, "Not with my conversation or touch." He lowered his voice and added, "Nor my mouth." He chuckled when Maria's eyes widened at his inference. "But with my eyes and my heart I will attend you, for I will watch you at every turn and love you with every breath."

"Then I can endure," she told him. "Until tomorrow is ended," she added. "How will I endure your absence?"

"Hush, pet," he said, forcing a smile. "The music is ending, and we are drawing too much attention for a lord and his ward."

The music did end, and Brock bowed to Maria as she curtsied.

"Lord Brockton Thorton and Miss Maria Castillo Holt!" the loud voice boomed once more. Maria resisted the powerful urge to reach out and take hold of Brock's arm as he walked away from her. But resist she did, knowing his heart was hers.

❧

The evening wore on with Brock charming the many debutantes in attendance and Maria politely accepting dance after dance with partner after partner. Throughout the evening and on into the late night hours, their eyes would meet spontaneously, and each would smile with joy in their secret knowledge of what would be.

Rebecca and her mother had departed at an earlier opportunity, and now the remaining guests were departing gradually as the hour was indeed late. Maria was grateful to be bidding them farewell, for her feet ached, her eyes burned, and her body longed for respite.

Suddenly, however, the attention of the departing guests was arrested by an uproar that burst from the entry hall. Angry voices were raised in shouting, and Maria recognized one of them as Brock's.

The musicians, remaining guests, Lady Thorton, and Maria all rushed out into the entry to investigate. There stood Brock facing a tall, immaculately groomed man who wielded a large bloodstained knife. Maria gasped when she saw the front of Brock's shirt saturated with blood.

"I will kill you, Brockton! High and mighty, Lord Brockton Thorton! Bah! You bleed like any other man," the stranger shouted.

"Get out! I'm warning you, Harrison. Else you'll die by my own hand!" Brock shouted.

Maria glanced quickly at Lady Thorton as she gasped and breathed, "Harrison!" The rosy blush emptied from the great lady's lovely face, leaving her as pale as death.

The violent man turned and eyed the great lady. "Well, Mother. Have you missed me?"

Lady Thorton fell to the floor in a stunned faint. Maria knelt, lifting Lady Thorton's head and placing it gently in her own lap.

"Leave now, Harrison. I'll not have you upsetting my mother," Brock demanded.

"Your mother? Your mother and mine, I remind you, dear brother. And who is this?" the intruder asked, gesturing in Maria's direction.

Maria shrank from him as he approached, as if the very essence of evil were intent upon her.

"My, my, my! You are a rare beauty," the man muttered. But as he reached for Maria, Brockton took hold of his coat collar, powerfully pulling him backward and throwing him to the floor.

"I'll not tell you again, Harrison. Leave here!" Brockton shouted, kicking the man hard in the midsection. "Pick him up and throw him out," he ordered two on looking coachmen.

"This is only the beginning, Brock! I tried to reason with you! Now you've had your chance and denied it! You will pay. And dearly!" the man bellowed as the two men escorted him forcibly through the front door.

Several women fanning Lady Thorton were whispering, and Maria was astounded at their revelation.

"Harrison Thorton!" one woman exclaimed. "I cannot believe it! I was certain some ill fate had befallen him and he lay dead in the dirt by now."

"He deserves no better, that one," the other said, nodding.

Maria stared at Brock. She wanted to run to him and inspect his wound, but as he spoke she forced her feet to their place and waited.

"Forgive us, friends, for the unfortunate experience. Please, please accept our thanks for your attendance. And do not let Harrison spoil your memories of the evening," he said.

Brock stood at the door and shook the hands of

each departing guest. Then he bolted it and instructed several of the maids to assist Lady Thorton to her chambers.

When at last the entry was abandoned, Maria could restrain herself no longer and ran to him. "Brock! Oh, Brock! There is so much blood!"

He tore off his coat and shirt and dabbed at the wound with them. "It's nothing. Believe me, where Harrison and I are concerned, this is nothing more than a scratch," he grumbled.

Maria took his hand and led him to a small room near the entry. It housed a washbasin and towels used for guests who wished to refresh themselves. She closed the door and hastened to the basin, filling it with water from the pitcher. Quickly she soaked a cloth in the cool water and turned to apply it to the wound.

"Oh, Brock!" she cried in a whisper as she lifted his arm to bathe the wound. It began at his left side just under his arm and traveled down diagonally across his torso and stomach.

"It's a scratch," he protested, though he jumped each time she pressed the cloth against his injured flesh.

As Maria cleaned the wound, her attention was drawn to Brock's artistically sculpted chest, arms, and shoulders. He resembled a statue she had once seen at a museum as a child. His chest itself was wide and muscular, his shoulders straight and broad, his stomach a solid mass of muscular definition. Maria was fantastically unsettled and looked up to see if Brock had noticed her sudden discomfort. However, he had his arm raised and was inspecting the damage done him.

"This will no doubt cause me great annoyance for several days to come," he grumbled, looking down at her then.

"No doubt," she mumbled awkwardly, pressing a length of fresh, dry cloth to the wound.

Brock was not one to overlook an opportunity to tease, and well Maria knew it. Chuckling at the blush on Maria's face, he asked, "What do you think, my pet?" He ran one hand slowly over his own chest.

Maria cleared her throat, turned, and began folding his discarded shirt. "I think he must be a dreadful person."

"No, not him. About this scratch. How do you think it appears?" he asked.

Maria cleared her throat again but did not turn to face him. "I think it appears exceedingly painful."

Brock chuckled. "Actually, it is not so deeply cut, now that I look at it. What do you think, Maria? Do you think it will heal quickly?"

Maria still did not turn to look at him. "I would think so. You certainly appear to be…healthy. I am quite certain it will heal in due time."

"Define healthy," he whispered into her ear.

"Healthy, Brock! Quit…quit teasing! Healthy. You know very well what I mean. I had better check on your mother," she stammered. She turned to leave, but Brock caught her arm, somber once more.

"Did she talk to you about my leaving?" he asked.

Maria cast hurting eyes to the floor. "Yes. But I do not see why it is necessary," she lied.

"Oh, you do not?" he laughed, turning her to face him. "Women are a true mystery, dear Maria. You see, it is not in the least unsettling for you, seeing me thus… standing before you only half-clothed. ButI, beholding you simply standing there fully dressed, am greatly… agitated. That is why it is more than necessary. And now there is Harrison to deal with as well."

"I cannot bear it if you leave," Maria whispered, gazing up at him. Her thoughts held no questions concerning the strange man who was apparently Brock's brother. All she could consider was the knowledge of his impending absence.

"You will bear it better than either of us would if I stayed. I must away," he said, taking both of her hands in his and raising them to his lips. When he released them, she did not let them fall from his face but rather caressed his neck and laced her fingers together behind it.

"Who is this brother of yours, and why have I never heard of him?" she asked as she felt his hands encircle her waist.

"Do not concern yourself with Harrison. I am to be your only concern," he whispered, smiling.

"You are and ever shall be my only concern," Maria muttered just before their lips met.

He pulled her snugly against him, and the warmth from his body burned through her entire being. His mouth was heated, moist, and enticing, and their kisses soon burned into a passionate exchange.

He broke from her for a moment and gazed into her sapphire eyes. His hand cupped her face gently, and, smiling, he whispered, "You do see the necessity of my leaving?"

She dropped her own gaze. "Yes," she muttered as tears spilled over her cheeks. "Though I cannot believe you would ever—"

"Each man knows which temptation might break him, kitten," he said, pulling her into his arms once more. "I cannot believe I could be so bewitched by a child," he mumbled into her hair.

"I am not a child," she reminded, nestling against him.

"I know. I meant when you were. When you were that flirtatious, raven-haired baby who captivated me so many years ago."

All at once, the feeling of security Maria had experienced since beginning her life at Thorton Manor abandoned her entirely.

Looking up into Brock's exquisite face, she asked, "Who is this Harrison?"

An expression of deep concern crossed Brock's features then, and he released her.

"My brother. Disowned, disinherited, and despised by my father many years ago. He is the elder of we two. I have always feared he might return when Father was gone," he growled.

"He frightens me, Brock. He owns such obvious hatred and resentment toward you."

Nodding, he said, "Think no more of him. He will not trouble us further."

But Maria did doubt. Something deep within her was unsettled. She involuntarily shivered.

"Now, you go before Mother finds you in here with me. She will shoot me herself if she finds us thus," he said, smiling at her.

Maria forced a smile and turned to leave. She paused, her hand on the door latch. Without turning around, she said, "I love you, Brock. I always have… from the very first moment." Without waiting for a response, she fled from the room and up the stairs.

Maria knew she must look in on Lady Thorton. It had been so apparent the incident with her disowned son had extremely distressed her. She knocked softly on the door to the woman's chambers.

"Is that you, Brock?" came the near hysterical reply.

"No, milady. It is Maria," she answered.

"Oh, my darling! Come in at once! At once!"

Maria opened the door to find Lady Thorton sitting in the midst of her bed, sobbing. Immediately, she went to her, embracing her.

"Oh, milady! I am so sorry! Please, do not carry on so," Maria pleaded as her own tears began to trickle over her cheeks.

"Oh, my darling child!" Lady Thorton said, looking up and taking the girl's face firmly between her elegant hands. "I am sorry this had to happen tonight! Your coming-out!"

Maria smiled. "Nothing could have ruined this day for me, milady. As you well know."

"Oh, Maria, what joy you bring to me!" Lady Thorton sniffled and brushed tears from her cheeks. "And to know that…well, I could not be happier either…now that you have reminded me. So much happiness to look forward to," she said. "I will not dwell on the painful past."

"Yes," Maria said. "Let us think only of the future, milady." The future meant belonging to Brock and owning him in return. Yes…Maria would think only of the future.

❧

Surprisingly, Maria fell asleep with ease once retired to her own bed. The events of the evening wove heavy fatigue, and she did sleep. Visions of Brock lingered in her dreams, and she did sleep.

She was awakened in the early hours of the morning. While darkness still owned the land, before the sun became its proprietor, he came to her.

"Maria?" came the whisper very near her ear.

Her eyes opened slowly to find Brock leaning over her, smiling. His handsome face before her, she smiled up at him. In the next instant, however, realization entered her tired mind, and she sat upright in her bed.

"Oh, no! You're leaving!" she exclaimed in a whisper, tears instantly filling her eyes.

Brock nodded and put a finger to his lips to indicate she should speak quietly.

"When will you return?" she asked in a frantic whisper.

"It is not certain. I…I will write," he whispered as he reached out and twisted a lock of her hair around his finger, a frown puckering his brow.

She threw aside her quilts and stood before him. She reached out and took hold of the lapels of his greatcoat. "Do you promise? I shall die…I shall literally pass from this very life if I'm not to hear from you!"

He cupped her tender cheek with one strong hand and said, "I promise it."

She brushed a tear from her cheek but did not move to embrace him.

"I love you, Maria," he whispered. He took her face between his two capable hands and drew it to his own, his kiss moist, fierce, heated with molten passion.

Maria locked her arms around his neck as they kissed, silently vowing never to release him. He was life to her now. He had been life to her for so long. How could she let him go?

All at once he broke the seal of their lips, burying his face against the soft flesh of her neck for a moment.

"Release me now, Maria," he breathed.

"I will not," she whispered, tightening her embrace.

"Release me now, or we will both be lost to the ruination of irresistible passion," he grumbled, pushing her away.

"Brock…you would never…" she began, but he

closed his eyes and held up a palm to beg her to stop.

"I…I can no longer…I can no longer be certain I would not," he said, shaking his head. "And you but sixteen and so…so…"He looked to her then, simultaneously frowning and smiling. "You will belong to me one day, Maria," he said. "One day I will not have to leave you." He turned and angrily strode from the room.

He was gone. Maria felt all at once cold, alone, frightened, and miserable.

"Two years," she whispered, brushing the tears from her cheeks. "An eternity it will seem to me."

Returning to her bed she wept until the first rays of yellow sunlight peeked in through the window. But no sun's bright beam could brighten a day where Brock was not to be near.

$\mathcal{B}$ETROTHED

Brock did not remain away from Thorton Manor for merely weeks. Neither did he remain away for merely months. Lord Brockton Thorton remained afar for an entire year! A year he was gone, a year in which Maria dreamt of him every day and night, waking or sleeping. A year in which she tried to busy herself with her stitching, her music, and accompanying Lady Thorton on charitable visits to Brock's tenants. An entire year in which she dreamt and planned and waited—waited for the beloved day when Brock would at last return, take her in his arms, and smother her with his delicious kisses.

Maria's greatest joys during the long, agonizing, lonely year were the letters she received from Brock. She received a letter from him weekly or more often, and she herself wrote nearly each and every day. His letters became her breath, her very life and hope in life. Maria did not know how she would have existed without Brock's letters, his constant reassurance he loved her, would return to her, dreamt of owning her for his own.

And now, at long last dawned her seventeenth birthday and Brock's anticipated return. A grand event had been coordinated by Lady Thorton in order to announce Maria's betrothal to Lord Brockton Thorton, and in anticipation of it, Brock was en route to Thorton Manor.

Brock was expected to arrive at any moment, and Maria's entire body was plagued by knots and nerves. Letters were one thing, face-to-face quite another. Had he changed? Would he still feel the same toward her? Certainly his letters told her he loved her, professed his misery without her. Yet what if his feelings had changed? Would he still be agreeable to the betrothal? It seemed silly and somewhat disloyal to doubt him. Yet she knew what a profound example of an ideal man he was in feature, form, ethic, and spirit. Would he find great fault or flaw with her upon seeing her again?

Maria opened the bottom drawer of her vanity and removed the last letter she had received from Brock, dated six days before. Once again she read to herself the last words of the letter.

...and it seems like forever since I stole a kiss from you last. Therefore, prepare yourself, kitten...for upon my return one week hence, I am fully intent upon savoring

the flavor of your mouth! Not that mere days of tasting you would near ever content me...

    Forever Yours,
    Brock

Inhaling a deep breath of resolve to be courageous and faithful in his loyal feelings, Maria clutched the letter to her breast and whispered, "I know he loves me. I know he must."

The morning was slow in passing, and soon the hour for midday meal had come and gone as well. Maria tried to occupy herself at reading a book in her chambers. But it was difficult to concentrate, and she found herself having to read the same passages again and again and again.

Then at last, and as if in a dream, she heard on the breeze the rhythmic pounding of hooves. Leaping from her chair, Maria rushed to the window. Yes! At last! She could see him approaching at a strong gallop. Brock!

Only moments later he reined his mount to halt beneath her chamber's window. As he looked up and smiled at her, the sheer magnificence of his presence, the utter beauty of his person, lifted her. He did love her! It was greater evidenced in his eyes than even in the words of his letters, and Maria felt her confidence beginning to return.

"Hello," he greeted, chuckling. "And who might you be, pretty miss?"

Maria smiled, beaming with delight at the sound of his voice, his playful teasing.

"I?" she asked, feigning innocence as she placed a hand to her bosom. "I am merely the chambermaid here, milord. I am just now airing this very room."

"Ah," Brock said, nodding. "I do not often make a habit of abducting beautiful women…but in your case, miss…I will more than happily spend years in prison if only for the opportunity at seducing one such as you."

Maria giggled with delight at his flirting. "Brock," she sighed, smiling.

"Here," he said, tossing a parcel up to her. "Happy birthday, kitten."

Maria caught the parcel even for not being able to take her eyes from her beloved. Had he changed? She thought not so much. She fancied his shoulders were broader, his face more handsome. Yet he was Brock still…her own Brock.

He smiled again, and she watched as he rode toward the stables. Then, with a squeal of delight, she tossed the parcel on her bed and turned to view herself in the looking glass. As always, she was dissatisfied with what she saw there, but with a quick smoothing of her dress and pinch to redden her cheeks, she turned, dashing from the room.

Reaching the top of the stairs, she halted. "Now, calm yourself, Maria. Descend in the manner befitting a lady," she whispered.

However, when she had less than halfway descended the staircase, the large front doors swung open, and Brock stepped into the entry. Instantly,

Maria's lingering, ladylike decadence turned to the more familiar rapid plunge downward to greet him.

Brock chuckled and caught her securely in his brawny embrace as she threw her arms about his shoulders.

"You're home, at last!" she whispered, unable to stop her eyes from filling with joyous tears.

"Are you happy to see me then?" he whispered, nuzzling her neck. Maria gasped at the thrill, the utter euphoria washing over her at the sense of his touch. Her mouth began to water, and she wanted nothing more than to let her lips find his.

"Yes," she whispered.

Her knees weakened and then buckled when she felt his lips brush her neck. He drew back, and she gazed into his captivating eyes. He smiled, causing his boyish dimple to appear as he caressed her cheek with the back of his hand.

"Time is quickly ticking, Miss Holt. Surrender to me now, or I shall force upon you my intentions of ravaging you," he whispered.

His words took the very breath from her bosom; she felt her cheeks go crimson with the blush of desire.

"Your…your mother is about, milord. No doubt she has already been notified of your return," she whispered, breathless in his arms.

"All the more reason for haste, eh?" he said, taking her chin firmly in one hand and tilting her face upward as his descended toward it.

He squandered no time in bestowing soft, teasing

kisses but instead kissed her solidly on the mouth with such potency it near suffocated her. As his mouth devoured hers in heated passion, Maria fancied her own overwhelming, feverish desire might actually give way and render her unconscious. How had she managed to survive an entire year without his touch, his kiss… without him?

"Brockton Richard Thorton! Release that girl at once!"

Startled at the sound of Lady Thorton's insistent order, Maria broke the seal of their deepening kiss and cast her eyes to the floor.

"Brockton, such behavior! Dear boy, the betrothal has not even been announced as yet. Control yourself!" Lady Thorton scolded, lowering her voice.

"Now, Mother," Brockton consoled, releasing Maria and gathering his mother into an affectionate embrace while placing a tender kiss on her forehead. "I've not seen Maria for an entire year! You must allow my behavior where she is subject may be a trifle… incorrigible."

Lady Thorton smiled at her dashing son. "Incorrigible? Savage may better term it." The older woman looked from Maria to her son and back. "Five minutes, Brockton. Only five minutes. After this, a chaperon will be necessary at all times. Understood?" Lady Thorton whispered.

"Understood. Completely unwillingly. But understood…just the same," Brockton muttered, returning to Maria and capturing her in his arms once again.

"For pity's sake, Brock. Privacy! Not here in the entry for all the world to see!" Lady Thorton reprimanded.

Maria stood in awe. Was Brock's mother, the ever proper and respected Lady Thorton, actually suggesting her son, Lord Thorton, proceed with his previous endeavors?

"Yes, of course, Mother. You're quite right," he said, chuckling. Then releasing Maria, he took her hand and began pulling her toward the small room adjacent to the entryway.

"Behave, Brockton. Do you hear me?" Lady Thorton called after them.

Having bolted the door behind them, ensuring their complete privacy, Brock turned to Maria. He grinned mischievously and winked at her. Maria drew in her breath suddenly. For the very first time, she began to feel somewhat anxious in being alone with him.

"I've missed you," he said, standing before her.

She looked up at him and then quickly away. Suddenly, the realization of what an indescribably handsome man he was disturbed her. She felt in that moment as if she were once again the child of thirteen he had found cowering behind a door so long ago. How could one such as he truly find anything attractive or loveable in such a simpleton as she?

"You're jarring my confidence, Maria. Have you, upon seeing me again, suddenly found me inadequate in some way?" he asked. She looked up quickly to see him frowning and completely sincere in his question.

"No! How could you even ask it?" she stammered.

"You've rather the look of uncertainty about you," he said.

"I only wondered…" she began.

"Yes?"

"I only wondered…if you perhaps you were concluding the very thing upon seeing me again," she whispered.

She heard him release a relieved breath.

"Do you think my mother would find it necessary to let me…compromise you, as it were…for an entire five minutes had my feelings toward you lessened in any respect?"

She smiled and shook her head shyly.

"Very well then. You have your answer," he said. "Now, to further assure you that I truly love and treasure you, and not only your immortal beauty, I shall refrain from pawing at you for the remainder of the time allotted me." He folded his arms securely at his massive chest, planted his feet solidly to the floor, and stared straight ahead. "Now," he said, "yell me what you've been about for this past twelve months."

"Oh," she began, feigning indifference. "Dreaming of you, mostly."

His face very nearly broke into a smile for an instant, but he continued to look past her.

"I see. Excellent usage of time, as I see it," he said. "What else?"

"Oh...and wondering if your kisses were truly as pleasant as I remembered them to be."

"Pleasant?" he exclaimed, frowning down at her. "Why not cute? Sweet? Common? Passable?"

"I see we still have our ego intact," Maria giggled.

He reached for her then and drew her to him. "And our talents," he whispered as he bent to kiss her.

"That is wonderful to hear," she whispered. He took her mouth with his then, kissing her thoroughly, fiercely passionate. She melted against him, careless of his rough whiskers, abrasive against the tender flesh around her mouth—careless of his powerful embrace forcing the frantic breath from her body—careless of anything save the feel and taste of him.

After a time, he took her face between his hands, tipping her head backward as he rained tender kisses along her throat.

"Had I not gone away, Maria," he whispered, "I promise you...the cost would have been your virtue and—"

"Ssshhh," she interrupted, placing a hand over his mouth as he gazed into her eyes. "You do not credit your honor enough, Brock."

He pushed her hand from his mouth as he said, "You credit my honor too highly, kitten." He smiled as he studied her face, brushed a strand of hair from her forehead. "You've changed," he said. "I cannot believe it as you stand here in my arms...yet you are even more beautiful than when I left."

"I have not changed much, sir," she told him,

unable to pull her gaze from his mouth. She swallowed hard, trying to restrain the desire to kiss him again.

"Oh, but you have," he said, still looking at her. "You look…and do not take offense…still you look older somehow." A delightful thrill swelled within Maria at his utterance. She wanted to look older, to appear matured enough to attract and hold such a man as stood before her.

"We have but five minutes, Lord Thorton," she told him, tracing the outline of his lips with her fingertips. "Do you truly prefer to spend it in light conversation when your mouth could be otherwise occupied?"

She smiled, pleased with herself when his mouth fell agape, his eyebrows raised in delighted astonishment at her flirting.

"Not…not if I've an invitation to…" he stammered.

Maria placed her index finger on her lips, pressing it then to his. "Here is your invitation, Milord Thorton," she whispered. "Do you accept?"

"Vigorously, milady," he breathed. "Most vigorously."

His kiss was hers again then—heated, moist, and unrestrained.

❧

"My dear friends," Brock began, "I am euphoric at the opportunity to announce to all of you good friends… that a boundless blessing has been bestowed upon my most undeserving self."

A hush fell over the mass of guests. Maria felt her

face flush as all eyes began to settle to where she sat at Lady Thorton's side.

"It has been allowed that, on this very date one year hence, I am to be the luckiest of men. For it is proud I am to tell you now...of my impending marriage!"

There was a veritable roar of clapping, laughter, and good wishes. Heads bent together in knowing speculation, and Maria felt her blush intensify. Lord Brockton Thorton was about to announce his betrothal to his ward. She knew it was in everyone's mind.

"Come now, friends," Brock said, chuckling and motioning for the crowd to quiet once again. "Am I to understand it is so unashamedly obvious to each of you who my intended might be?"

"'Tis obvious to us all, milord. 'Tis the fair Miss Holt!" came a shout from one of the men. As Brock nodded in confirmation, more cheering commenced.

He held one hand toward Maria, and she placed hers in it. She stood, her knees trembling and weak with delighted anxiety. As she gazed up at the dashing young man who would be her husband, her mind whirled. How could an orphaned child such as she come to such a great bounty? It was as if she were living a fairy tale!

After the extravagant meal at which Brock had announced their engagement, the ball commenced. Maria stood next to Lady Thorton as she received well-wishes and congratulations from guest after guest.

"Oh, my dear. What a beauty Brock has captured," one elderly man said as he stooped and kissed Maria's hand.

"A treasure like none other," another said.

Maria began to feel burdened by the compliments, for she knew she was the one infinitely blessed at having one such as Brock for her own. And when she thought she could endure not one more lavish compliment, Brock returned and begged a dance with her.

At the very sense of being held in his arms, she again slipped into a state of complete euphoria.

"What is it?" he asked, smiling lovingly at her.

"Am I truly to belong to you? It is certain this must be a dream from which I will dreadfully wake soon," she whispered.

He smiled and bent to whisper in her ear. "It is indeed a dream, Maria. One from which you shall wake in a year's time. And when you do stir from your slumber that blissful morning three hundred and sixty-five days hence, you will find the dream at present suffers immeasurably in comparison to the one that will be your very life's breath. For on that morning, Maria…you will awaken having slept in my arms."

Maria gasped and looked around quickly to ensure no one had heard him, even for his having spoken so softly.

"Brock! You mustn't say such things to me!" she scolded in a whisper.

"Why? Is it revolting for you to think on it?" he asked, winking at her. In truth, she found nothing more wonderful to imagine.

"Never…but someone will hear you, milord!" she answered.

Brock chuckled and continued to lead her in the dance. She became aware the dance was moving them closer and closer to the large doors leading from the ballroom to the gardens. And when she looked up, he was grinning impishly at her.

As she had supposed, once they reached the doors, he quickly took her hand and led her out and into the garden.

"I've not had a moment alone with you since I arrived three days ago," he said, holding her hand firmly in his as they strolled about the gardens.

"Your mother does not trust in our good judgment," Maria said, smiling.

"My mother does not trust that I still possess any good judgment," he corrected. "And with good reason, I admit."

They walked in silence for several moments before stopping at the most fragrant of rosebushes.

"I've something to give you," he whispered.

"A kiss?" she asked, smiling at him.

She was puzzled when he shook his head. He then reached into his pocket and withdrew a small box.

Understanding resplendently struck Maria, and she stared at the case as he opened it. At the vision of what lay within, she gasped, putting her hand to her mouth. The ring was extraordinary in its simple elegance. A single diamond was positioned in the middle of the golden band, three smaller gems, sapphires, at one lower edge.

"Did you think I would deny you a visible token of our betrothal?" he asked.

Maria could only stare at him as he removed the ring from its case and, taking her hand, placed it on the appropriate finger.

"It is…it is…entirely unnecessary," she whispered.

Brock reached out, cupping her cheek in his hand, caressing her lips with his thumb. "It's only a trivial token of my love for you…of my obsession, Maria," he said quietly.

"Obsession?" she repeated doubtfully.

"Obsession," he stated firmly. He traced her lips once again with his thumb and then said, "It is difficult for you to believe, is it not?"

She looked away shyly as he continued.

"Difficult because I am so much your elder, inheritor of a title and wealth. I am sure your mind has concocted other such ridiculous reasons for doubt as well. I know you." He took her face in his hands and forced her to look at him. "Know this, Maria Castillo Holt…I have no other passions in life, save you. I have nothing else in the world that I could not live without, save you. Wherever I may be, whether far away from you or holding your tempting form in my arms… my thoughts are of you. You doubt my terming you my obsession. Yet I tell you only this: it is what you are." He dropped his hands from her face and turned away, drawing in a deep breath and exhaling tensely. "I suppose you find me weak and lesser masculine for saying it. Most men are not inclined to bear their souls thus, so to speak."

She brushed a tear from her cheek and, reaching out, grasped one of his strong hands. "I love you, Brock. More than you can pretend to understand," she whispered.

"Obsessively?" he asked, turning to her, his adorable grin hinting to expose his darling dimple.

"Ever so much more than obsessively," she said.

Brock turned to her, his eyes traveling the length of her. He seemed to struggle with some inward battle, all at once finding victory.

A profound rapture rose within Maria's bosom as he took her in his arms, her throat the willing recipient of one soft kiss. She let her arms slip around him as she pressed her lips tenderly, lingeringly, against his throat in return. Brock straightened, instantly tense.

"I should take you in," he said.

"Yes. You should," she whispered, reaching up and letting her fingers tangle in his hair. He closed his eyes for a moment and inhaled deeply.

"We must return," he stated, yet he stood unmoving.

She nodded and whispered, "Yes. We must."

Brock bent, pressing his mouth to hers, kissing her with rough intensity. Though Maria found this kiss somewhat uncomfortable, nearly painful in a manner, still she reveled in it, thrilled by its complete power over her senses. She could believe him when he kissed her like this. Believe he loved her as obsessively as she did him.

"I must have one more drink of you first," he mumbled. "Endeavor to quench my thirst, Maria."

She smiled, her fingers once again lost in the softness of his hair.

"I cannot, milord," she whispered, "for my own mouth is dried out for want of yours."

"Maria," he breathed a moment before crushing his mouth to hers.

❧

"I was about to send someone out there to retrieve you, Brockton," Lady Thorton knowingly whispered upon their return to the ballroom.

"I only wanted to give her the ring, Mother. It should be a private gesture, do not you agree?" Brock whispered in response to the reprimand.

"Yes. And I am sure the redness and overall... um...condition of Maria's lips is due to her smiling so broadly at your offering it to her," Lady Thorton said, winking at Maria. "I'm not at all sure that it is wise to harbor the two of you under the same roof any longer."

"Two days more, Mother. And then you can breathe easier," Brock whispered.

Maria felt discouragement trying to creep in on her blissful evening. Two days! And he would be gone again! And for how long? Would he stay the entire year this time as well? Her heart stung, ached, pained her in every regard at the thought. She could not live another moment without him. She could not! And yet, to own him, she must. Still...how would she endure?

❧

For the two days following the ball, Brock and Maria accepted various invitations to luncheons, visited various tenants of Lord Thorton's property, rode for miles and miles, and kept as otherwise occupied as was possible. Each moment she was not in his arms found Maria anxious to the point of nausea over his impending departure. An odd sort of foreboding seemed to settle in her as well, and she wondered how she would bear his absence again.

A great despair settled over Maria as she retired that last evening, her only thoughts that when she awoke in the light of morning, it would be to find Brock already gone. It was torturous! Why had her father stipulated she be eighteen before she marry? She was sure if he could have guessed at what would be between them, surely he would not have made her age a factor of his terms.

❧

"Maria," came the whisper. She awoke instantly at the sound of his voice, the knowledge of his presence in her chambers.

Sitting up, she found Brock standing beside her bed. He was dressed for travel, and panic overwhelmed her.

"You will write to me?" she begged, her voice quivering with emotion.

"Of course," he whispered. "Now, be quick and see me off. Mother will have me beheaded if she catches me in here," he chuckled.

Maria threw aside her quilt and stood before him, aching to be in his arms.

"I correct myself. Mother would have me tortured to a long and miserably slow death," he said, studying her from head to toe. Maria knew she stood before him in only her nightdress, but it mattered not to her.

It was pointless to beg him to stay. Brock was, after all, an honorable man no matter what he professed to be in the intimate moments they shared. She knew he would do nothing to tarnish their reputations—or at least hers. Yet she was beginning to believe it was, indeed as he maintained, difficult for him not to touch her at every opportunity.

"Will you kiss me goodbye then?" she asked in a whisper.

He looked away for a moment and then, taking a deep breath, nodded. "Only if you promise to keep your fingers out of my hair," he said, smiling. "In fact," he added, "keep your hands from about me entirely." She frowned, not fully understanding. He continued, "You see, I'm leaving you now for possibly as long as a year." She nodded. "Your...attire...is somewhat... provocative. And I sense my power of will weakened... being here in your chambers. Do you understand me?" He was in complete earnest, she realized, and she nodded. "Very well. Goodbye, Maria," he said. He stooped, letting his mouth tenderly find hers.

The desire to reach for him was overpowering, and Maria locked her fingers together behind her back. He stood straight again and said, "Goodbye. When next we meet, kitten…I shall never have need to leave you again."

He bent once more and kissed her, more fiercely this time. Their kiss deepened, and he took her shoulders between his hands. Maria let her own hands clutch his powerful arms. Slowly she moved toward him until her body was flush with his and his arms held her tightly. His mouth left hers and traveled the length of her neck. His breathing had become uneven and labored. His kisses were hot and fierce on her flesh, and she clung to him, letting her fingers entwine themselves in his hair.

"Brock," she said as she sensed the risk of the situation. "Brock," she repeated, hoping he would be able to find the strength in himself to leave her—for she was certain her own strength was fast fleeing.

At once he released her, dropping to his knees. He took her hands and looked up at her. "It is my love for you, Maria. It takes possession of my senses. But know my wanton desire is fanned only because of the purity of my love for you." Maria knelt in front of him and let her hand caress his cheek, her heart breaking at the thought of his leaving her. He continued, "It's my love for you that keeps me from you as well. Do you realize it?"

"Yes," she whispered as the tears escaped her eyes.

"When I return, it will be to remain." he said. He stood at once and left the room.

Maria listened as the rhythm of Stetson's gallop grew fainter and fainter. Brock was gone.

$\mathcal{A}$LL IS $\mathcal{L}$OST

"Six months, my darling," Lady Thorton sighed, working the stitches on her linen. "Six months and this dreadful waiting will be at an end. Finally. I'll have you at last as my daughter, and Brock will be home to stay."

Maria smiled and set her book aside. "It seems like ever so long yet, milady. How will I ever endure it?"

Shaking her head, Lady Thorton smiled. "I do not know. But it is sure to drag on and on, is it not?"

Entering the library, the maid curtsied. "Milady, Mr. Jacob Peterson to see ya."

"Peterson? Well, send him in, Lillian. By all means," Lady Thorton replied.

Lillian curtsied again, and as Lady Thorton set her stitching aside, Jacob Peterson entered.

"Jacob!" Lady Thorton exclaimed.

Jacob Peterson appeared before Lady Thorton is such a state as Maria could never have imagined. He was completely disheveled. His hair was uncombed and his clothes wrinkled. He wore several days' beard growth as well, all of which was quite uncharacteristic of the ever-proper solicitor.

"Milady Thorton! Tragedy has come to you this day, and I've no way of diverting it!" he shouted.

Maria stood. The sensation of utter dread infiltrated her very soul and then threatened to drown her entire being.

"Jacob! Whatever do you mean? You're in such a state! I've never seen you thus!" Lady Thorton exclaimed. Maria could see the great woman was experiencing the same overwhelming anxiety.

"Vanished, milady! Presumed dead! That's what they are saying. I've searched for days, milady! He is nowhere on earth! Milady Thorton, what misery this will bring to you! I dare not expound. But I must." Jacob was truly in a state of near madness.

"What nonsense do you jabber on about, Jacob?" Lady Thorton asked, though Maria saw the tears forming in the grand lady's eyes.

"Lord Brockton, milady! Dead, they say! At the hand of thieves!" he shouted.

Lady Thorton dropped to her knees in disbelieving shock. Maria stood paralyzed.

"Where is he laid out?" Maria asked at last. She felt only horror, sickness.

"Nowhere, Miss Holt. That is just it. They do not know where he is."

"You see there, Jacob. He's alive! He is fine. Just put up somewhere," Lady Thorton rationalized.

"No, milady. I have searched. He is nowhere. And if it can be proven he came to his end, then…"

Lady Thorton buried her face in her hands and began to sob bitterly. Maria looked at Jacob, paralyzed with shock.

Jacob Peterson returned her gaze. He stated in a voice almost void of emotion, "If he can manage to have Brock declared legally dead…Harrison Thorton will inherit the title and all else left by his brother, being there is as yet no other heir."

"Harrison?" Lady Thorton gasped.

"Yes, milady," Jacob confirmed. "All is lost."

Maria still stood stunned by what Jacob was telling them. Her mind emptied of thought as slowly she began to walk forward.

"Brock?" she whispered. Lady Thorton and Jacob Peterson watched helplessly as she turned to them and said, "You are mistaken, Mr. Peterson. We are to be married in six months' time, Brock and I. He will be home then. He would not leave me to live my life alone without him."

She closed her eyes for a moment as a vision of Brock appeared in her mind. At once, an excruciating pain exploded throughout her entire essence. She found herself unable to draw breath, so great was the pain in her heart. There was only blackness then. Although she heard the noise and knew her body had become limp and fallen to the floor, she felt nothing before sinking into a deep, painful abyss where only darkness dwelt.

HOPE

Maria stood at her window. She stared out across the fields, out across the earth in its peaceful naïveté. As always, she looked down to the way leading to the manor house. As always, she closed her eyes for a moment and listened, strained to hear the familiar rhythm of Stetson's stride. But there came no drumming of hooves. There would be no handsome rider to rein his horse in beneath her window and lovingly smile up at her. There would be no parcel tossed to her and abandoned on her bed as she ran down the stairs to greet her love.

Three months had waned since the horrid day Jacob Peterson had come with the unbearable news of Brock's death. As Maria stood at her window, knowing this should have been the day he would have come back to her—the day he would have begun to settle the wedding arrangements—her broken, failing heart nearly ceased in beating.

Maria did not move from the window, even when she heard Lady Thorton enter her bedchamber.

Lady Thorton laid her hand softly on Maria's shoulder and said, "Come down and sup with me, darling." Maria did not speak. Lady Thorton frowned, stroking her lovely hair, gazing out the window with her. "You have been at this window for nearly nine hours, Maria. Please...come down with me now."

"Just a few more moments, milady. I promise," Maria whispered.

Lady Thorton sighed heavily. "Very well, my love. When you are ready then." And she respectfully left the girl to her own grief.

Life was only misery for Maria. She feared she would never be able to recover from the loss of her beloved. And now—now with Harrison in the house as well—there was many an hour she considered fleeing from it. Had it not been for her profound love and devotion to Lady Thorton, she would have found a way to leave weeks before.

Harrison Henry Thorton had arrived two weeks after Jacob Peterson's revelation of Brock's demise. He did not even attempt to feign sorrow for his mother's loss but simply began trying to intimidate his mother into giving him control of the estate and all the affairs with it.

Maria had been astounded and overjoyed at the strength and steadfastness of the great lady. She had managed to keep him from living at the house, though he frequently visited. Further, she was flaunting a superb ability in running the estate with the help of Jacob.

However, at the thought of Harrison, Maria shuddered. It was all too obvious what his thoughts were concerning her. He was a cruel, lustful man, and Maria saw this all too often whenever he looked at her. She always met his penetrating inspection with an air of courage and defiance, but deep within she shivered with fear and insecurity at his very presence. Yes, were it not for Lady Thorton, the situation would have been too unbearable, and Maria would have taken flight.

Looking longingly down the way one last time, Maria closed the window and left her chamber. Lady Thorton was still grieving as well, and Maria realized it had been quite selfish on her part to spend the day in futile dreaming.

"My dearest," Lady Thorton greeted her as she sat at the table. Lillian began serving them, but Maria's appetite was lost the moment Harrison walked into the room.

"Ah! My two favorite females!" he said confidently as he entered. "I shall be dining as well, Lillian. Serve me," he commanded, removing his riding gloves and sitting at the head of the table.

"Do not assume too many airs, Harrison," Lady Thorton stated.

"Oh, dearest mother…when will you accept the fact Thorton Manor and everything connected with it will fall to me at any moment?" he said, assuming heinous superiority.

"Do not conclude triumph as of yet, Harrison. Brock has still not been found," Lady Thorton reminded.

"He will not be found, Mother. He is dead. I assure you." The villain grinned knowingly.

Maria knew Harrison had killed Brock or at the very least had a hand in his disappearance. She knew Lady Thorton suspected as much herself, for they had spoken of it.

"And how is my little enchantress this evening?" Harrison addressed Maria.

She ignored him.

"Ah. Playing coy, are we, Maria? You, as well as Mother, had better set your mind on me...for Thorton and everything belonging to it...will be mine," he said, chuckling.

"You delude yourself on too many accounts, Harrison," Maria stated.

"How so?" he asked, amused.

"In the first state, because you will never own Thorton. In the second, even if you did, I do not belong to it. As for the rest...the reasons are far too many to enumerate."

His sudden laughter was boisterous and startled Maria. "Well, done! What a vixen you are, Maria! I dare say Brock had his hands full with you...somewhat literally too, no doubt. I shall look forward to the same."

Without looking at him, Maria rose. Walking to where he sat, she slapped him hard across the face.

122

His anger was provoked, and he roughly took hold of her wrist. "You'll pay for that, wench!" he growled, rising to his feet and glaring down at her.

She narrowed her eyes and met his stare.

"Do not touch her, Harrison. I'll have you severely dealt with if you do not unhand her this moment!" Lady Thorton commanded.

Harrison looked to his mother, sneering. Releasing Maria, he said, "Very well. I can wait for her submission to me."

"I have lost my appetite, milady. If you will excuse me," Maria said, making to leave.

"Beggin' yar pardon, milady," Lillian said as she set a plate heaping with food in front of Harrison. In her thick tone of the Green Isle, she continued, "There is an aged mother askin' far yar favor at the kitchen door."

"Very well, Lillian. Feed her a good meal, and have cook give her some coins from the jar in the kitchen. You should well know the routine," Lady Thorton said, somewhat puzzled at Lillian's even mentioning it to her.

Lillian looked nervously at Harrison, who had begun to devour the food before him.

"I think she be somewhat of an eccentric, mum. She's askin' far favor from the young miss of the manor. 'Tis Miss Holt she wishes to see, it is."

Maria was curious. Something was stirring inside her. Something…a feeling she could not quite place.

"I shall go, of course. Whatever could she want from me?" Maria asked.

"I do not know, miss," Lillian said. Yet Maria felt

Lillian did know something more than she was leading her to believe. She followed Lillian into the kitchen and found an ancient-looking woman seated at the table there.

"How may I serve you, old mother?" Maria asked, sitting across from the woman.

"Would the brother be about then, miss?" the woman asked in a heavy Irish accent.

"The brother?" Maria asked.

"That's what I be askin', lass. The brother. The elder...disowned I think he be," the old woman said.

Maria looked at the woman, and a frightening, anxious excitement began to rise in her.

"He's taking dinner just now," she answered.

The woman dropped her voice and said, "I've come to help ya, I have. To help ya help him."

Maria felt the hairs on the back of her neck prickle. "What do you mean?" she asked the woman.

"The younger brother...the rightful heir. Yar his betrothed, are ya not?"

"Brock?" Maria breathed, afraid she might faint from the mad hammering of her heart. "Yes. Yes, I am his."

"The sweet baby girl with the raven hair...his kitten...grown up and meant to be the mistress of this manor?" the old woman asked.

Maria gasped. Reaching out, she took one of the woman's leathery, knurled hands in her own.

"You have news of Brock?" she asked in a whisper.

"That I have, lass. But I'm to be makin' certain that the brother elder is not within listenin'."

Maria drew in several deep breaths in an effort to calm herself, in an effort to keep herself from fainting dead away.

"Lillian!" she whispered. "Quickly! Go stand at the door and tell me if Harrison makes to move this way."

"Yes, Miss Holt," Lillian said, nodding, her own eyes wide with excitement.

"Please. Tell me your news, old mother," Maria begged.

"They call me old Mother O'Malley, they do," the ancient woman began. "I live far from here and near Bevary Prison. I had a lad, me first...he died there. Lonely, cold, and without hope. So I visit them, I do. The prisoners. I see every one of them, but only about one time in a month. There is a prisoner there...kept in the deepest-most cell. They let me visit him, though I think they've been havin' orders not to be allowin' it. I've seen him thrice...though the first two he wasn't wantin' to confide in me. Distrustful was he."

Maria's heart was pounding so hard she thought it might stop altogether. But hope kept her from dying—the same hope she had secreted for months. Hope that Jacob Peterson had been wrong in his information about Brock's death.

"Well," the old woman continued, "five days ago, I went to visit him, I did. He's discouraged, that one. I asked him if he's things to discuss with an old mother. And...then he tells me it. He's Lord Brockton Thorton.

125

'Tis wrong doin' that's found him in Bevary…but not his own. An elder brother who covets what's his."

Maria knew well the tears streaming down her face. They had become as familiar as breathing. "Pray continue, kind mother," she whispered.

"Somethin' within me bosom told me this one is a gentleman…born and bred and honest. He told me, he did, of his concern for the girl to be his lover…wife…mother of his children. And also concern for his mother, who will be at the mercy of this demon brother. I was believin' him at once…and came here. Though I gave him no false hope of release…I be willin' to help ya free him. Me own boy died in there. And wrongly accused was he. Yar man is weak and wastin'. Horrible life it is in there, lass. He says ya've got a likeness of him that ya wear and that I can see it, and his story will be provin', it will."

Immediately, Maria lifted the locket she wore about her throat always and opened it, revealing the likeness of Brock.

"Yes, lass. That be the one. I speak the truth, I do. I swear it," the woman whispered.

Maria clutched the locket tightly to her bosom and tried to steady her breathing. Alive! Brock was still alive!

"You must accompany me there," Maria begged.

But the old woman shook her head. "No, lass. 'Twould then be clear to the authorities who helped ya. No. I'll leave. Ya come later, and I've a plan, I do. For liberatin' the handsome lad."

$\mathcal{B}$EVARY

Maria was awash with guilt over lying to Lady Thorton. Still, she could not give away any false hope to Brock's mother or risk Harrison's finding out by any means. As she sat in the coach watching the landscape pass, she tried to remain calm. What if it were all a deception? What if it were not Brock wasting away at Bevary but a cruel trick?

Harrison had questioned Maria and Lady Thorton on Maria's destination.

"She needs a holiday, Harrison. Though you may care less than not for your brother's death...Maria is heartbroken," Lady Thorton had told him.

Harrison had, of course, been against Maria's taking a holiday. Yet Maria guessed it was in an effort to win some sort of approval from her that he stepped aside and allowed her to leave. She closed her eyes, trying not to think of Brock's evil brother. In her mind, she saw Brock—saw him asleep across from her in the coach that had carried them from her aunt and uncle's cottage and to Thorton Manor so many years before. She saw his smile, his dimple, the impish spark that leapt to his eye each moment before he kissed her.

Praying for his safety, praying he still lived, she opened her eyes as the coach jolted. Maria had escaped, and now, with the help of Mother O'Malley, Brock would be with them again soon. She knew it would be true. It must be true!

Carefully, she reviewed the strategy in her mind as the coach traveled over the countryside. Mother O'Malley had gone over it in every detail so Maria would be sure of what she was to do.

As Maria sat thus, reviewing the scheme, uncertainty crept over her. Was she, Maria Holt, capable of accomplishing such a feat requiring such steady deliverance and step? She was not certain of herself. But she must be! She must, for her own sake and for that of her beloved Brock. She would be strong. She would prevail. And she would spend her nights lovingly held in Brock's strong arms. She would!

❧

Maria dipped her fingers in the ashes of an old fire outside Bevary Prison. The fires that produced them had long since died out. No doubt their flames had warmed many a cold and lonely guard.

She smeared the ashes on her cheeks and forehead and under her eyes, finally wiping her hands on her already dirty and ragged clothing. She was trembling, nearly uncontrollably. What if she were found out?

What would they do to her? Yet as she approached the guard at the prison's front gate, she pulled her cloak's hood over her head, thoughts of herself only secondary.

"Good day, old mother," the guard said, nodding and moving aside for her to pass.

"Good day," she muttered as she passed him. Her heart was pounding so furiously with fear she was sure he would hear its mad drumming as she passed. But he simply stepped back to his post.

Hurriedly, Maria entered the dark, cold, oppressive edifice. Several more guards, filthy and foul-smelling, nodded and let her pass. With each challenge met and conquered, she grew more confident and more impatient. The prison was damp, and the stench permeating every passageway sickened her. Maria held her cloak more tightly against her mouth and nose as she hurried through the dungeon-like corridors, at last reaching the furthest cells.

The light from the flamed torches flickered ominously, and she began to sense doom and despair. Tears filled her eyes as she thought of her precious Brock locked up in one of the horrible Bevary prison tombs.

At last she found it: the cell the old woman described. She knew she had only one opportunity. If she had been mistaken, taken one false turn, all hope would be lost for Brock and for herself as well. She had no doubt of it.

She motioned to the guard to unlock the iron door imprisoning whatever man she might find inside.

Maria watched anxiously as the guard inserted an enormous iron key into the lock. She jumped, startled, as the lock groaned and gave way with a loud knock of iron against iron.

"He's a lively one, that one in there, mother. Watch yourself," the guard warned as Maria stepped from the corridor into the shadowy, filthy, frigid cell. The slamming of the enormous door behind her sealed her within the stone vault.

For a moment, she remained motionless as her eyes attempted to adjust to the gloom of darkness in which she stood. One high, barred window allowed a solitary shaft of sunlight to permeate the miserable abode. Dirty straw was strewn on the floor and, to one side, two well-worn, tattered quilts.

Her disbelieving gaze fell to the furthest corner of the room. There, sitting on the floor, arms resting on knees, head resting on arms, sat a pitiful figure.

Maria's heart beat madly! Tears filled her eyes, fear her heart. *Surely, this cannot be he*, was her first thought, for the shell of a man appeared emaciated, dirty, unshaven, and weak.

"I've no wish for a visit today," came the raspy, yet undeniably familiar voice. He spoke without looking up.

Maria's hand flew to her mouth to muffle a gasp as tears flooded her cheeks. She must remain calm! She must not raise the suspicion of the guards.

As slowly as her body would allow, she walked

softly toward him, saying, "Come now…let a lonely woman find comfort in a visit."

She stopped her approach when he lifted his head and demanded, "Who are you?"

She raised her finger to her lips, indicating he should be silent. "'Tis I…Mother O'Malley. Come to visit, as I do every month, lad."

Maria hastily moved toward him as he stood and shouted, "Who are you? Your voice…it sounds to me…I've finally lost my wits, have I not?"

Quickly, she moved to him. She placed her fingers to his lips as she dropped the hood that had hidden most of her face.

"No, my love," she whispered. "You are as witty as ever."

She smiled as she looked up into his beautiful, beloved eyes—the eyes she had dreamt of for so long. A shaggy, matted beard covered his face. Although his hair hung well below his shoulders, it was his hair— beautiful chestnut-gold flecked hair unique only to Brockton Thorton! The tears streaming down Maria's face only increased as she saw the hollowness of his cheeks and eyes. His lips were dry and cracked. Looking at him, she could see how thin he had become. Fury at those who caused him such pain and suffering erupted within her!

"Maria?" passed the raspy whisper through the parched lips. His eyes narrowed, and he reached out, wiping at the ashes on her face with thin fingers.

"Shhhh!" she said softly.

"What goes on there, old mother? "the guard queried from beyond the door.

"Not a thing, lad," she answered in her best mimic of Mother O'Malley's voice. "The lad was dreamin' for a moment. He'll be fine, he will. Now, let us be havin' our words." She sighed with relief as she heard the guard's retreating footsteps.

"Maria," Brock breathed, reality finally penetrating doubt. The moisture in his eyes increased. "My pretty kitten," he whispered, his voice breaking with emotion and fatigue.

Maria looked back to the cell door to ensure their privacy. She let her arms carefully encircle his waist as she endeavored to embrace him. She was aghast to sobbing at how thin he was. He held her to him. She sobbed bitterly when she realized he was too weak to hold her with the strength he once had.

"Brock," she wept ever so quietly, "you're here! I've found you!"

A moment later, Brock dropped to his knees, his arms encircling her waist. His head fell forward against her stomach. He buried his face in the folds of her dress, and she let her fingers be lost in his hair. He shivered, and she fancied for a moment that he was close to something akin to sobbing. She did not find his emotion weak, for she could not fathom the horror he had endured over the past months. Further, she was close to fainting herself, so great and overpowering was her joy in feeling his touch once more.

Sensing he may be too infirm to rise again, she

knelt before him, his eyes again meeting her own. For everything he had endured, his eyes still captured her soul, her obsessive love and desire for him overwhelming her. Every essence, every pore of her being was alive in him once more.

"Maria," he whispered again as he raised one hand to caress her cheek, attempting to smile.

Carefully, for fear she may cause him unnecessary pain, she took his bearded face in her hands and whispered, "Really, Brock. Such dramatic lengths to go to…simply to avoid losing one's bachelorhood."

He puffed a single chuckle. It seemed to be all that was in him. Maria smiled and adoringly stroked his beard.

He said then, "You are in grave danger, Maria. You must leave at once!"

She shook her head and whispered, "Not alone. Never again will I be without you."

"Do not be foolish, girl," he growled. "I am in no condition to execute any form of attempt at escape. If they find you here, they will…" His words trailed off and vanished. He seemed undone at the touch of her satiny lips to his cheeks.

"I will not exist without you again, Brock," she whispered. She moved to kiss his mouth, but he turned away.

"No," he mumbled. "I have no looking glass in which to sight my condition. Still I know what a devil must sit here before you."

Maria's heart tore with pain. How many times in

her life had he come to her rescue? Even saved her life? How many times had he salvaged her self-esteem and confidence? How many times had the situation been the reverse, with her feeling drab and plain in comparison with the magnificent lord of the manor?

She took his face between her small hands and turned it to hers once more. She asked, "I have come all this way, and you do not even want to kiss me?"

He rolled his eyes, and her heart leapt at the sight of the all too familiar gesture. "It is not a question of whether or not I want to kiss you, temptress. Look at these lips! The very flesh of them dry, parched. What do you expect me to—"

Again his words were halted by her endeavors. Brock seemed to watch in disbelief, unbelieving and mesmerized as Maria slowly moistened her own lips with her tongue. His eyebrows rose in wonder as she then placed one finger on her tongue and used the appendage to moisten her lips further. She smiled playfully and moistened the finger once more. This time she placed it on Brock's lower lip.

Instantly she was in his arms! His solid embrace was once again kindred to what it once was. Although his heavy facial hair scratched at the tender flesh of her face and his parched lips no doubt ached against her own, the tears of ecstasy flooded her cheeks.

Brock's kiss! Nectar to her senses! The physical strength may well have been drained from him, but his unconscious ability to send the blood hastening through her veins was as overwhelming as ever it had been. More so!

He kissed her as he never had before, with a desperation and loving brutality, threatening to overpower her virtue and sanity! Her mind fought to regain control of their desperate situation, of the reality of it.

Pushing herself from his arms, she put a hand at his mouth to keep hers from returning to it.

"We must go, Brock. At once," she whispered.

"How?" he asked, collapsing back to sit in the straw. He was breathless, weakened from the effort at loving her. "You've a plan then?"

"Yes," she whispered.

She quickly explained what action they must take, but he frowned. "I am greatly weakened, Maria," he said as she helped him to his feet. "Still…to have you in my arms again…to take you to wife, to bed, and to my life…for that I may muster even what was once within me," he whispered.

Maria wiped the tears from her cheeks, desperately wanting only to be in his arms once more. Still, until escape was their success, it could not be.

Maria took a deep breath. Brock nodded and doubled over to feign illness.

"Guard!" she cried. "Quickly! Come in here this minute!"

The heavy iron door opened, and the guard lumbered toward them.

"What's all this, old mother?" he asked.

"The lad has taken ill with stomach pain," she said. "See here. He's bleeding as well, he is."

As the guard bent to inspect his prisoner, Brock looked up and muttered, "Hello, Petey."

"What?" the guard asked, astonished.

Brock took the guard's shoulders, bringing his knee up with an incredible force to meet with the man's stomach. The guard fell to the floor, gasping for breath. Brock hit him squarely on the back of the head, rendering him unconscious and falling to his knees from the exertion.

"Here," Maria said, reaching beneath her cape and producing rope. "Help me to remove his clothing and then bind him. We must be quick."

The possibility of impending freedom seemed to rejuvenate Brock. Maria watched as he donned the guard's dirty clothes and then tied and gagged the beast. Leaving the cell, they made their way up through the corridors, returning the greeting nods of the other guards they passed along the way. Maria was very grateful for the dim-lighted, shadowy state of the prison corridors.

As they approached the front gates, however, the guard posted turned and looked at them, curious.

"Ay? What goes on here?" he asked as they approached.

"She's hurt her ankle," Brock said, imitating the guards' roughened language.

"You all right now, mother?" the gatekeeper asked.

Maria nodded and motioned him aside.

"I'll see the ol' woman home," Brock said as they left by way of the Bevary Prison front gate.

Slowly, they ambled down the lane, Brock pretending to help Maria walk as she limped. Once around the bend, they wasted no time in rejoicing at their escape but continued on in a quick manner, trying to appear unsuspicious.

Several minutes later, they reached the home of Mother O'Malley. She was waiting for them.

"There be a horse out back for ya, sire," Mother O'Malley said in a whisper. "Me own dear lad, Michael, will see ya safely back to the inn, lass," she said to Maria.

"How can we ever thank you? How can such a debt ever be repaid?" Maria asked through her tears. The enormity of it all—the truth of Brock's escape, of his very breath and life—was washing over her like a beloved spring rain. It was strenuous, and she felt the need to collapse. Yet there was not time for weakness of mind or body.

The woman smiled at her. "'Tis no debt, I tell ya. His lordship was not meant to be there in the first."

Brock raised the old woman's knurled hand to his own parched lips. "We are forever indebted to you, good mother. Remember it. When you need help of any sort, you will call upon me. I am your servant, ma'am."

The woman nodded, and Maria smiled at the woman's blush.

"Go on with ya now. They'll be ridin' here at any moment," the woman whispered. "First, you'll be tyin' me to the kitchen chair there. I'll say the lass came and stole me clothes to break ya from that hole."

Brock nodded. He worked quickly, and soon the old woman was tied comfortably to the chair. She assured them if it took the guards at the prison too long to find her, her son would find her when he returned from taking them to the inn.

Brock changed clothes, as did Maria, and they rushed to the rear of the cottage. Brock mounted the horse tethered there. Maria looked up at him. He was almost vibrant looking.

"I'll not be able to return home for some time, Maria," he said.

"What?" she gasped. "Brock! I cannot possibly—"she began.

"I will have to prove this crime of Harrison's first. The declaration will have to be circulated I do not belong in prison. I promise I will come to you the moment I am able."

"Brock! Please!" Maria began.

"I love you, Maria," he said. He reached down, taking her chin roughly in his hand. Bending toward her, he kissed her once more. Then with a snap of leather, he was off at a gallop.

Seated in the carriage and headed for the inn, Maria explained to herself that Brock had no time to dally. He had to escape, put distance between himself and the prison before he was found missing. Yet somehow she felt lonely and lost, frightened and defeated. He'd been away from her for so long. The evil of suspicion, the devil's tool, doubt, began to whisper to her thoughts. Perhaps his feelings had changed. Men did change during long, horrid incarcerations. No! Brock loved her. She knew he did. She had seen it in his eyes in the cell when he recognized her. Had she not?

The carriage stopped, and she alighted. She nodded at the old mother's son and dropped several coins into his hand. She endeavored to appear calm as she entered the inn. Upon seeing her, the innkeeper broke immediately into a babble of local news.

"Oh, miss! We're so glad to see you've returned safely," he exclaimed.

Maria feigned ignorance. "Why? Whatever for?" she nonchalantly asked.

"Such news! One of the convicts from the prison has up and simply walked out! He's still in these parts, no doubt!"

Maria put her hand to her mouth in a dramatic gesture. "No! How horrid! How frightening!"

The innkeeper nodded vigorously and continued, "A mean one, they say. Killed someone, they say."

"No! How terrifying! A murderer? Unleashed in the township?" she gasped.

Again the innkeeper nodded.

"Well, I've no wish to stay here a moment longer! Imagine, cutthroats and thieves roaming freely about! When does the next conveyance leave?" she asked, fanning herself dramatically.

"A wise decision, miss. A wise decision."

❧

Two hours later, Maria sat in a coach as it raced toward home. As she gazed out the window, she whispered, "Is he well?" Where was he? Would she ever see his face again or feel his fascinating, loving kisses? Would she ever be his wife?

How difficult it would be not to tell Lady Thorton she had actually seen Brock! Touched him! That he was, in fact, living! Yet she knew it would be far too dangerous. One mistake, one simple word at an evening meal attended by Harrison, could be catastrophic if anyone but she knew of Brock's liberation from the prison.

Would he indeed return? she wondered. People changed drastically after enduring such atrocities. Would he still desire to live the life he had desired before? Would he want to live it with her? The utter elation and relief that had flooded her being upon their exit from the prison walls were fast turning to doubt and despair. Still, Maria shook her head. Closing her eyes, she thought of Brock, sensed his arms about her, his lips pressed to hers. She saw his smile, his beloved dimple, his eyes. In these visions, the devil was beaten, and affirmation he loved her warmed her once more.

❧

"You look far worse than you did upon leaving for your holiday, my darling!" Lady Thorton exclaimed upon Maria's entering the house.

"Simply fatigued from travel, milady," Maria lied as the beloved woman embraced her.

"Harrison is about," Lady Thorton warned in a barely audible whisper.

"Ah! Maria! Are we quite rested and recovered, my sweet?" Harrison's voice boomed from behind her, sending a sickening sensation throughout her body. It was as if the mere whisper of his name conjured up the devil himself.

Maria turned, glaring at him.

"I see you haven't lost the sorceress's look in your eyes. Good to see it!" he chuckled.

"The child is tired, Harrison. Leave her be," Lady Thorton stated.

"Mother," Harrison began, "I have been very patient with you…tolerant of your assumed air of matronly authority. But I warn you…curtail it! The time is upon you when I will be listened to and obeyed here. I am in charge of matters of estate…and in charge of you."

Maria was tired and infuriated. Her words lashed out at the brute. "You are the most vile, loathsome creature ever to draw breath, Harrison Thorton!" she shouted, moving to stand before him. "It is no wonder to me your own father disowned and forgot you. To treat your mother so! And to despise a brother who never wronged you!"

She watched as Harrison's face went crimson with fury. "How dare you speak to me so!" he growled.

"I shall speak to you in whatever manner I see fit!" she replied through clenched teeth.

"A brother who never wronged me, you say?" he continued. "You foolish chit of a girl! Brockton

141

wronged me at every turn. He was born to begin with! Father doted on him, though I was the eldest and heir."

"You were the bad seed, Harrison. Do not deny it," Lady Thorton interjected.

Harrison chuckled. "Ah yes! 'The bad seed'…'the black sheep.' Be that as it may, I am the eldest. I chose to live my life as befitting an heir to a great title and estate. But Father was bent on morality and honor! Constantly, he tried to mold me, as it were, into what he had been. Into what dear brother Brock was becoming. But I would have none of it! High moral code, ah! Honor? What good is it, I ask you? If you've wealth and position, what necessitates honor…morality?"

"You're truly sickening," Maria mumbled, unable to comprehend such thinking.

Harrison burst into boisterous laughter. "Sickening, am I? Brock and I…we're of the same blood and bone, Maria. How is it you found nothing vile and unattractive in my younger brother?"

"You may be of similar physical ingredients. But you are not the same in mind. Nor in opinion, nor passion, nor—"

"Passion, you say? Well, my little novice…what know you of passion? Please…do not try to intimate Brock was capable of passion! I know my brother too well. Straight as an arrow and far less lethal!"

Maria was provoked. She raised her arm, intending to slap him squarely across the face. Realizing her intention, he caught her wrist in one hand.

"Now, now, Maria. Let a true man of passion demonstrate the emotion," he mumbled.

Then, before she could move, he had captured her in his arms and was consuming her tender lips with his own. With every ounce of strength within her, Maria broke from him. She felt as if she might vomit as she looked up into his face that now appeared more hideous than before. She spat on the floor at his feet, attempting to rid her mouth of his memory.

Rather calmly, Lady Thorton approached Harrison. Her eyes narrowed as she said, "If you ever dare to touch her again, Harrison, I will cut your throat myself."

Harrison chuckled. "Reconcile your mind to seeing such displays, Mother. I plan to have everything I deserve. Everything," he said, lewdly smiling at Maria.

"I would die before I let you lay a hand on me again. I will not be taken in surprise, in any manner ever again!" Maria snapped sharply.

"Do not lay wager on it, my dear," Harrison growled. He turned and left the room, calling to them as he went. "I'll be in for dinner tomorrow, Mother. Please be sure the servants are notified and prepared."

"Maria, my darling! I...I am so very sorry! I had guessed his intentions were as much...but still I hoped..." Lady Thorton began.

"He is mad, milady," Maria whispered.

"Yes, my darling. I believe so."

Maria looked at Lady Thorton then, surprised at her own ignorance. She had been drowning in such deep despair, had been so miserable, she never before inquired as to the reasons for Harrison's disowning. "Was there one act…one deed in particular that caused Lord Thorton to abandon him? Or was it merely an all-encompassing character?" Maria asked.

"He tried to kill his younger brother. Repeatedly," Lady Thorton pronounced.

Maria gasped, her mouth gaping open in astonishment as she looked at the grand lady.

"Brock was always a good boy," Lady Thorton continued. "He is seven years the junior to Harrison. Harrison was ever the disobedient, immoral, expectant heir. When he was the age of twenty and Brock thirteen, Harrison realized their father favored his younger son. What father would not, I ask you? I favored Brock as well. He was good, compassionate, and chaste. Harrison was not. The first instance occurred while they were out hunting together. Brock was accidentally shot in the leg. Or so Harrison related the story. Then Harrison endeavored to push Brock from a high cliff ledge. We were suspicious…but he was our son! It was inconceivable that…" Lady Thorton dabbed at the tears in her eyes. "One morning, Richard came upon them arguing in the stables. Harrison shouted to Brock he would see him dead, one way or the other. It was affirmation…horrid affirmation spoken from his own lips. Richard disinherited and disowned Harrison that very night. Brock's life was threatened. Do you see? How could we permit Harrison to remain? He threatened, indeed he had tried…to murder his own brother," Lady Thorton said, weeping.

Maria could sense the grand lady felt a terrible guilt at having abandoned a child. "It was need be, my lady. A brother who would plot to murder? To murder in any regard! But to murder his own brother? There was no alternative," she comforted.

"Yes. I know. No alternative."

Maria embraced the woman, all the while her mind spinning with the horror of it all. She was more frightened than ever. Closing her eyes, she silently prayed for Brock's swift return, for her safety and Lady Thorton's until he did.

"Hurry, my love," she whispered. "Make haste… lest we are all of us lost to his evil intent."

FOR WHAT SAKE BORN

There came no word. No message. Not one. Nothing from Brock. For three months there came nothing. Maria began to lose hope, to fear some terrible fate had befallen him—something worse than imprisonment in Bevary. Perhaps he had been ill at the time of escape and his condition had worsened. Perhaps thieves had set upon him. Perhaps Harrison had received news of his escape and finally succeeded in murdering him! Perhaps something had taken him, and he was lost— forever lost.

In the dark, lonely hours of midnight, her mind plagued her with worry and anxiety and whisperings to her his heart had changed. Brock had found another in his travels since escaping Bevary; Brock had found comfort in the arms of someone else. Had a strange woman found him ill and beaten, nursed him to health, and won his heart? So many nightmares, waking and sleeping, began to plague Maria. She thought she might expire of their torment. Yet she rallied in the brightness of morning and sun. Each day she managed, somehow, to regain her hope, her courage, her knowledge that Brock was on his way to her rescue. Each day she managed to exist—exist in the hope of seeing him once more, of being held in his arms.

Harrison was growing irritable and impatient. His solicitors had been unable to acquire the estate and title rights for him. Without sufficient proof of Brock's demise, he could not inherit. He was anxious and, at times, violent.

Apparently, Lady Thorton's warning to Harrison so far as Maria was concerned had some effect on him. Even though he ogled her mercilessly, insinuating lewd improprieties with his glances and grins, he had not touched her again.

Yet this day, something was wrong about the very air. This day, Maria was uneasy. This was to have been her wedding day—her eighteenth birthday. This was to have been the day she would be given to Brock and he to her. But now, as she walked about the garden where Brock had given her his ring the night of their official betrothal, she was filled with dread, fear, and an endless, empty loneliness.

"Pondering what might have been, my sweet?" Maria turned to see Harrison standing just behind her.

"Leave me be, Harrison. I've no desire to look at your hideous snout this evening," she said.

He chuckled and took several steps toward her. Usually Maria stood her ground firmly when he approached trying to intimidate her. This time, there was something about his expression—something frightening, unsettling.

"Leave me be, Harrison," she said as she felt an overpowering dread heightening within her bosom.

He chuckled. "Your father meant for you to be married on this day, did he not?" he mocked.

"To Brock," she reminded.

"To Lord Thorton's son!" he bellowed. "And so you shall be. We would not want to ignore your father's dying wishes, would we now, Maria?"

She turned, intending to run, but he caught her around the waist. Then, lifting her, he dropped her over his shoulder.

"Stop this!" she screamed. "Release me, Harrison!"

He chuckled and began walking toward the house. Maria beat on his back with her fists, pinched him, and kicked him unceasingly, but he was too powerful. He had her. Panic caused her to lose rational thinking.

As Harrison entered the house with his prisoner flung over his shoulder, Lady Thorton came running down the stairs.

"Release her, Harrison! At once! Do you hear me? At once!" she shouted.

Harrison strode to his mother and stood glaring down at her as Maria paused in her struggling. Surely Harrison would succumb to Lady Thorton's command.

"Do not interfere with me any longer, Mother!" he shouted.

"You will unhand her, Harrison. You will unhand

her, or there will be consequence," Lady Thorton said.

Harrison sighed with irritation as he growled, "Very well then. The both of you will learn this day who is to be obeyed in this house!" Maria gasped when she witnessed the beast strike his own mother with the back of his hand, knocking her to the floor.

"Stop him!" Lady Thorton cried, trying to stand. "Stop him!"

Several male housemen entered upon hearing the outburst. Reaching into his coat pocket, Harrison Thorton produced a pistol and threateningly aimed it at the men.

"Now…pursue this no further…or it will answer," he commanded. The men were undaunted until Harrison pressed the muzzle of the gun into Maria's rib. "It will answer," Harrison repeated as he continued ascending the staircase carrying Maria.

"Help me!" Maria screamed as she looked at the bewildered and helpless faces below.

Harrison laughed as he reached the door to one of the upstairs chambers.

"You realize what this is, do you not, Maria?" he said. "It is the bedchamber shared by the lord and lady of Thorton Manor." Maria tightly closed her eyes and struggled with all her might as Harrison fumbled with a large iron key produced from his pocket.

She was successful! She fell to the floor. She was free from his hold! She opened her eyes, glancing about to discern which direction would ensure her escape. It was then she realized why Harrison had released her.

"Brock!" she cried, looking up to see Brock struggling with his brother.

"You shall pay with your life for touching her, Harrison!" Brock growled, ripping the pistol from his brother's hands.

"No, little brother. You shall pay with yours for ever bringing her here," Harrison retorted.

"Miss Holt!" Jacob Peterson exclaimed, taking her hand and pulling her to her feet. "Has he hurt you?"

Maria could only shake her head in response. She was overcome with the scene unfolding in her wake. She watched as Brock's fist repeatedly struck Harrison's body. The blows were powerful and devastating, and the villain soon crumpled to his knees.

Harrison knelt on the floor at the feet of his brother, gasping for breath, his face a mass of blood and quick swelling. He looked up at Brock, who stood over him drawing angry breath.

"You've broken bones here, brother!" Harrison accused.

Brockton shook his head, and Maria thought of his weeks and weeks of incarceration at the hand of his elder brother.

"Better it would have been for you if I had broken your neck, Harrison," Brock growled.

Maria watched as the constable and two other men came forward and bound Harrison's hands. The men pulled him to his feet. He winced as one of them jabbed him in the ribs.

"Answer me one question, Brock. You owe it to me," Harrison panted.

"I do not owe you anything," Brock growled.

"How did you escape? You must have had help. You could not have escaped Bevary alone. How?"

Brock stood silent for a moment. Then he said, "You should have paid less notice to Father's wealth and position and more to the daughters of his dear friends."

Harrison looked to Maria, his eyes flaming with anger and indignation.

"You!" he breathed. "That...that infernal holiday mother allowed you to take."

Maria looked to Brock, but his eyes stayed fixed on his brother.

"Mother?" Harrison said in a pitiful voice as the men began dragging him down the stairway. Lady Thorton straightened, turning her back on her eldest son. Maria's heart ached for the woman. The pain and guilt evident on her face were agonizing to witness.

The moment they had gone, Brock went to his mother. She fell into his arms, sobbing. Maria watched for a moment but felt as an intruder eavesdropping on something very private. She quietly walked to her own chambers, closing the door behind her as tears blinded her. Weakened, she leaned against the door, still stunned by what had occurred and Brock's timely appearance.

Suddenly, there came a knock at the door. Maria startled as the vibration of the knocking rattled against her back. Her heart began to hammer, perspiration gathered at her temples, and her knees and arms felt weak. She managed to brush the tears from her cheeks, overcome by the certain knowledge it was Brock's fist against oak.

"Y-yes?" she stammered.

"May I enter?"

She drew in her breath and held it, undone by the mere sound of his voice. She could hear the lack of confidence in his words, and she knew the moment had arrived—the single moment of truth when all her fears would be vanquished or realized. Had nothing changed between them? Or had everything changed between them?

"Yes," she managed to answer.

She turned, stepping away from the door. As it opened, Brock stepped into the room. Her eyes beheld him, strong, healthy, and brutally beautiful once again. His strength and health had returned. Maria's heart began beating wildly. She fought with all she was to restrain herself from flying at him, begging for his embrace.

"It has been unspeakable for you, has it not?" he stated. "Living with Harrison's presence...his threats, no doubt?"

She could only cast her gaze to the floor and nod. He came and stood directly before her, and she could feel his stare at the top of her head. Still, she could not look at him again. For all her courage at Bevary, for all her bravery, what now found her so weak and fearful in his presence?

"I've come to apologize, Maria. For failing you," he whispered.

She looked up quickly, questioningly. "What?"

"You know I have failed you," he said, frowning. "I was not here to be your protector. I left you to the wolf, so to speak."

"You were imprisoned, Brock," she said. Had he gone mad and forgotten?

"That is what I speak of. I was truly pathetic. Weak to fall into such a trap."

"He had you put into Bevary Prison, Brock," she reminded.

He nodded. "Perhaps. Yet I should have anticipated such an act of treachery. I know Harrison well enough."

Maria could only shake her head. What was he saying? That it was his fault alone he had to endure such atrocity? She looked away as he took one of her hands in his own. His touch was stimulating to her senses, and she shivered with delight from it.

"I…I am giving you the choice, Maria," he whispered. "You are free. You have no obligation to marry me…the pathetic weakling you had to deliver."

"Brock!" Maria gasped as panic began to wash over her. Was he ridding himself of her just as her nightmares had caused her to fear? Would he leave her?

"Or," he continued, his eyes smoldering with emotion, "or I have brought the curate, and he waits downstairs."

"What?" Maria whispered, confusion mingling with hope in her bosom and brain.

"Today was to have been our wedding day, was it not?" he asked. "I leave the choice to you—your freedom…or the curate."

Maria looked deep into his eyes. His chest rose and fell with the labored breathing of restrained emotion. He yet wanted her! She could see it in his eyes! It was only his guilt, his feelings of failure, keeping him from embracing her—keeping him from embracing her and more. He loved her as much as ever he did! It was there, blatant on his face, in the set of his clenched jaw, in the sweet syrup of his eyes. He was only doubting his own worthiness of her, not his love for her.

She smiled, and a perplexed frown puckered his brow. Reaching up, she ran her fingers through his chestnut and gold flecked hair. He closed his eyes a moment, breathing a heavy sigh. She raised herself, kissing him tenderly on the chin. For a moment, he clenched his eyes shut more tightly.

Maria let her small hands caress his powerful arms, feeling the smooth and solid contours of his muscles. She was pleased he wore a short-sleeved riding shirt, so she had this opportunity to caress him thus. In an instant, his arms went around her, pulling her body against his own. His mouth found her throat, and she felt she might melt into nothingness at the satisfying sensation.

"You are coming downstairs this minute, girl, and we will be married at once! You will be mine, and I will have you at every turn! Do not resist, or it will go badly for you," he mumbled as his mouth took hers in a fierce and driven, eager and licentious kiss.

"Maria? Brockton? What is going on in that room?" Lady Thorton asked from beyond the door.

"Lord Thorton?" Maria whispered after he had enraptured her mouth with impassioned kisses for several moments more.

Brock sighed heavily, and she marveled at the relieved expression now dominating his features as he looked at her.

"What is it, milady?" he whispered, kissing her forehead.

"I think you had better answer your mother. She sounds a bit unsettled," Maria whispered, smiling up at him. He chuckled. "And then," she continued, "I think it would be wise for us to meet with the curate forthwith."

"And why is that, Maria?" he said, placing a heated kiss on her neck.

"Because then my Lady Thorton can go about her own business and…"

"And I can go about mine," he whispered in her ear.

Maria let her arms go around Brock's neck, pulling him tightly to her. He was there in her arms, alive and well and blessedly hers! Tear trickled down her cheeks as she inhaled the scent of him, felt the warmth and power of his body, of his existence.

"I love you, Brock," Maria whispered. "Oh, if you only knew how perfectly I love you!"

"You had better love me, kitten," he said, "for I

love you more than life. And...I intend to keep you a prisoner forever...in my arms."

"Truly, Brock?" Maria asked, wanting only for his mouth to take hers once more.

"Truly," he said, sweeping her into his arms. "But first, my love...we must away for a visit with the curate, else the constable returns to clap me in irons for such endeavors toward you that are not yet honorable."

"It is ever I have dreamed of this moment with you, Brock," Maria said, caressing his face with the back of her hand.

"Then I shall grant your dreams, Maria," he said. "Every one."

❧

"At last!" Lady Thorton sighed, dabbing at her tears with a dainty handkerchief as the curate ended the marriage ceremony.

"I...I am yours now, am I not?" Maria whispered as she gazed up into the handsome face of Lord Brockton Thorton.

"You are," Brock said, gathering her into his arms and melding his mouth to hers.

"Brock!" Lady Thorton scolded. Upon witnessing the depth of passion springing from the kiss her son was bestowing upon his wife, she glanced around at the smiling faces of the on-looking Thorton Manor staff. "Brockton Thorton! You are not in private as of yet!"

"I will soon alleviate that particular impediment, Mother," Brock said, lifting Maria into his arms.

"Brockton! Such behavior!" Lady Thorton

exclaimed, smiling as Brock carried Maria toward the stairs.

Brock closed the door to his bedchamber, letting Maria's feet fall to the floor.

"You are every wish I ever had come true, Brock," Maria whispered as his mouth toyed with her neck, placing tender, lingering kisses there.

"It is how the heavens meant it to be, kitten," he whispered as her fingers became lost in his hair. "For, above all else, I exist to adore you. And you, Maria," he continued, his mouth a breath from hers, "were born for my sake."

To my husband, Kevin...

My heart's desire,
My every dream come true,
The love even *I* could never have imagined!

And now, enjoy the first chapter of
Shackles of Honor
by Marcia Lynn McClure.

CHAPTER ONE

Life had always been that of immense privilege for Cassidy Shea. Her father, Lord Calvert Shea, was a dominant figure in society. He was popular in the most desirable of circles not only because of his fantastic wealth and titled position but also for his profound physical attractiveness and unique good nature. Cassidy's mother, Cylia St. Martin Shea, was also immeasurably well received. She was of excellent breeding, an erudite and magnificently gifted hostess, and also very beautiful. Cassidy's elder brother, Ellis Martin Shea, was well educated, quite astoundingly handsome, and groomed to perfection, ready to accommodate his father's mantle of title and position at any given moment. It was obvious and often said that the Sheas of Terrill were the finest of families—from all outward appearances well bred, happy, and content.

For Cassidy Shea, life could not have been more perfect from birth through her present seventeen years. Everything was delightful, every need provided for— every day without major tragedy or other undesirable incident. Her coming-out, for instance, had been glorious, grand, and indescribably successful. And she had immediately been bombarded with a barrage of handsome and worthy young suitors in the year and few months since.

Still, in spite of the family's popularity and glory, the perfections of the house, stables, and gardens of Terrill, and all her father and mother's attentions—the like of which many wealthy children were stripped, having been laid in the arms of nannies and governesses since the days of their births—it ever seemed to Cassidy that something lurked among the quiet corners of life at Terrill. It felt eerie, as if all truths were not perfectly tangible. For there had been times, especially of late, when she came upon her mother, a woman renowned for her command of emotions, dabbing at her eyes with a handkerchief or her needlework. Times when her father stood at the library window gazing out across the gardens, book in hand and open, yet never reading one solitary word upon its pages.

It appeared to Cassidy that these times of unrest, of secret sorrow or worry, had increased since her own coming-out. It seemed that each time a young suitor was admitted into the parlor with her and her mother for a short visit, her mother glanced almost regretfully at Cassidy, as if she were somehow pitying her young daughter.

Ellis went about his life as casual and carefree as ever. He had no greater concern at times than whether his stallion were the fastest in the county. He never seemed melancholy, and Cassidy wondered if perhaps he was ignorant to whatever it was that seemed to unsettle her parents in rare and quiet moments.

The incidents of concern apparent in her mother's countenance gradually escalated. As a result, one cool, late afternoon in spring, Cassidy found herself standing before the large looking glass in her chamber studying her appearance—the color of her skin and form of her body—wondering if perhaps she were stricken with some ghastly disease of which her parents had kept her ignorant.

She didn't appear to herself as if she were disease-stricken. She had her father's rather plain, unexciting hue of brown hair. Still, it was long, soft, and tinted with red highlighting when the sun caught it just so. Her complexion was her mother's—porcelain smooth, fair, and flawless, save for the small and subtle brown mole just above her upper lip on the right corner of her mouth. Her nose was of normal shape and size, her chin not too pointy nor too flat, her cheekbones high with just the right amount of pronunciation. Her eyebrows matched the color of her hair, and her eyes were a rather common shade of hazel. Her eyes were one of her glories, for they were perfectly almond-shaped and shaded by long, dark, almost ebony-black eyelashes. Feeling satisfied with her head, for she had heard it said in quiet whisperings that she was considered nothing less than at least very pretty, she turned to study her shape and form at a sideways angle in the glass.

It was true—she was not overly tall. Neither was

she too short. Her height measured five feet three inches—a height to be proud of, her mother told her. And her figure, though rather more buxom than she would have preferred but by no means abnormal, was quite well proportioned. Her hips were small but well curved, and her waist measured an enviable eighteen inches.

Turning to face the glass straight on once more, she frowned and sighed. She looked normal, but each time her parents studied her of late, there came an expression of regret of some sort across their faces.

Cassidy had only just stretched out her arms to her sides to assure herself regarding the straightness of her bones when Ellis stepped into the room. He leaned against the doorframe and folded his arms across his chest, studying her with an amused grin.

"Go away!" Cassidy ordered, irritated at his intrusion.

Ellis ran a confident hand through his rather mussed auburn hair and asked, "Are you simply drowning in vanity, dear one? Or can you offer some other explanation for your infatuation with that looking glass?"

Cassidy rolled her eyes exasperatedly and shook her head. "I said, 'Go away.'"

"But I have news. And I think you will want to hear it." Ellis smiled mischievously at his sister, his eyes fairly twinkling with the flicker of a secret cached.

"Let me guess. Is it something astoundingly

profound, dear brother?" Cassidy asked, turning from the glass to look at him.

"Oh, astoundingly," he teased.

"Such as…you have found a more efficient way of combing your hair?" she mocked.

"No. Not quite so important as that," he answered. "And anyway, my hair is in perfect order as always, dear one."

Cassidy sighed. She loved Ellis, dearly loved him. But he sometimes seemed so incredibly shallow. So…so lacking in brute masculinity. Not that he was feminine by any means, but he was too polished somehow.

"However," he continued, "you will have to cut short your little tête-à-tête with Gavin Clark, for we are having the most important of visitors in to dine with us this evening."

Cassidy's eyes blazed with aggravation toward her brother. She absolutely despised the way he teased in such a condescending manner about Gavin.

"Gavin Clark is more of a man than you or your lavender-scented friends will ever be, Ellis!"

Immediately Ellis dropped his mocking expression, replacing it with that of apology for teasing his sister. "I am sorry to tease you, Cass. I know how well you think of him, and he is a fine young man. But…but, Cass… you know that Father would never approve of it. Gavin is common, after all. They will marry you to a titled man and no other. You know that."

"I do not know it," she argued. "*You* carry the weight of expectation, not I. I often pity you, Ellis, for

I know what is expected of you. But surely Mother and Father would not present me to some elderly, bald, red-nosed old lord simply because of titles…which, by the way, are becoming more outdated and less important by the moment. They would not subject me to the same hopeless fate as Marietta Longswold's parents did her."

"Perhaps not. But they will not allow you to be given to a common fellow such as Gavin all the same."

Cassidy knew that Ellis truly loved her and cared for her feelings. She appreciated his efforts to prepare her for life. "I have not said that I wish to be given to Gavin Clark, now have I?" she reminded, smiling reassuringly as she took her brother's offered arm. "Now, do tell me—as you escort me out to the east lawns to meet my common beau—who is this astounding visitor who will be joining us this eventide as we sup?"

"That is the astounding part of it, dear one. I don't know." Ellis shrugged his shoulders when Cassidy looked up to him inquisitively.

"Come now, Ellis. A mystery visitor? There has never been such a thing in this house. Not since I've been old enough to evoke memory."

"As I said…that is the astonishment. Neither Father nor Mother will reveal his identity to me."

"That *is* astonishing," Cassidy muttered to herself. Suddenly an involuntary shiver trickled through her body.

"Someone been planting lilies in your grave dirt, Cass?" Ellis asked teasingly.

But Cassidy could not dismiss the foreboding feeling. As she walked quickly toward the east gardens and Gavin, she could not rid herself of it. And as she considered the recent fate of her dear friend Marietta at having been literally given in matrimony to old Lord Rapier, her parents deeming him a suitable husband simply because of his title and wealth, she certainly could not induce the sense of impending doom to evaporate. Even when she saw Gavin sitting on the bench under the large black oaks of Terrill's east lawns, she could not be rid of it.

Gavin stood and smiled as she approached. *Oh, he is handsome*, Cassidy thought to herself. She often wondered how she held his interest at all, for he was nearly twenty and she only seventeen. Yes, he was ever so handsome—and so rugged and strong! Gavin was a hard-working young man, wise in the things that young men couldn't learn in university. How could any woman prefer a man who was weak-minded in such things as those wherein Gavin was wise? Or weak in body for that matter? And Gavin had wit—a wit that most young men in whose company she found herself could not begin to understand, let alone emulate.

As Cassidy approached him, she marveled again at the handsome state of her secret suitor. He stood tall, broad-shouldered, blue-eyed, and blond-haired. His face and arms were bronzed from hours of hard work outside, and his smile was like drinking in a warm mug of wassail at Christmastime.

"Cass!" he greeted as she rushed into his muscular

embrace. He hugged her warmly, then held her away for a moment as he studied her, and said, "You are so beautiful."

"And you are far too flattering, Gavin," she scolded, though she loved his compliments. What woman wouldn't? "But I should not let you embrace me so, for it is completely improper, you know." She smiled and hugged him quickly once more before taking his hand in hers and leading him in a casual stroll toward the nearby gardens.

"So," he began as they meandered along the garden paths among the bright yellow of daffodils and lavender of crocus, "what tales of adventure do you have to recite to me today, my beauty?"

"Ha!" Cassidy exclaimed, throwing her head back in a giggle. "Adventures? Me? Ah, yes. I do remind you of the great ones, don't I? Joan of Arc? Guinevere? Yes, my life's excitement far surpasses any they could have known."

"Come now, Cass. Surely you have some news that you're wanting to share," he prodded.

Cassidy felt the cold chill trickling down her spine once more, and her thoughts were drawn to the news that Ellis had divulged to her mere minutes before.

"Well," she dropped her voice secretively, "we're having a mysterious guest in to dine with the family tonight."

"And a fine horse he sits for certain. I've only just seen it on my way here."

Cassidy looked to Gavin quickly. "What do you

mean *he*? And where would this be that you've seen him, and how would you know that he's meant to be our guest tonight?"

"I said I had seen the horse he sat, not he who rode it. And it was in your own stables just now. A magnificent bay that puts your brother's black to shame."

"Impossible! Ellis's stallion is insurmountable in his perfection," Cassidy argued.

"Not anymore. I could take you to the stables to see the bay…but we may be seen together and then—"

"Then take me. I'll only just pretend that we happened upon each other if we're discovered."

Cassidy's hands began to tremble unexpectedly as she followed Gavin to the stables. First her hands, then her arms, and then her very soul. Something was lurking in the shadows of the future. She felt it, but she could not identify it.

She tried to concentrate on Gavin's words as they walked, but she found herself preoccupied by the secretiveness of her parents concerning the guest. Never had they behaved so before, and she began to worry on various things. Perhaps her father was in financial ruin and had hidden it from them for years. Perhaps the guest was appearing to cart him off to debtors' prison and throw the rest of the family out into the elements. Or perhaps it was a famous physician come to break the news to Cassidy of the ghastly disease that would soon lead her into a torturous death.

"Well, there he is, Cass," Gavin announced as they entered the first building of stables. Pointing toward an enormous, wild-looking bay stallion, he added, "Magnificent beast, that one."

"Beast is exactly the thing," Cassidy commented. The horse was indeed beautiful but held a fire in its eyes as untamed and frightening as perdition itself. As she and Gavin approached the animal, it snorted, rearing up and neighing frightfully in its stall. It dug mercilessly at the straw beneath its feet and shook out its magnificent mane furiously.

"Oh, no, Cass! That's an animal of pure and untainted breeding, of exceptional grooming and care. A true gentleman's mount," Gavin marveled.

"Why not a woman's?" Cassidy asked, more desperate to minimize the importance of the evening's dinner guest than to defend the worth of women.

"This horse isn't tended to by merely a stablehand. Someone has spent hours in the breaking and grooming of it. And besides, he has the look of being just broken. A woman…most women would not feel safe with such an animal supporting them." Gavin looked from the horse to Cassidy, who was still staring at the animal in awe. "You've captured my heart you know, Miss Shea."

Surprised by the sudden change in the conversation, Cassidy looked up to see Gavin's mesmerizing blue eyes gazing admiringly down at her.

"You do flatter me far too often, Gavin," she scolded.

"I speak only the truth to you. I…I must beg a favor of you, Cass." Cassidy felt her heart begin to pound wildly, for she sensed the essence of the favor, and it caused her to feel delightfully unsettled in her stomach. "I would ask...I would beg the gift of one sweet taste of your lovely lips, milady."

Finally, she thought to herself. She'd waited so long for her first kiss. For Gavin's kiss. And now, at long last, the moment was upon her. Slowly he placed his strong hands, one at each of her shoulders, pulling her closer as his head bent toward her own. Then, delightfully at first, his lips caressed hers tenderly. His kiss was soft and sweet, pleasing to the senses in the first moments. But as his lips continued to linger on hers gently, she knew that this was not what she had always dreamed it would be. Her heart did not soar. Her spirit did not jump with elation. And when the mad pounding of the bay stallion's hooves on the stall wall and his violent neighing startled the very essence of Cassidy's senses, she broke from Gavin, pushing herself from his arms and backing further away from the frightening animal.

"He's only just anxious to be out," Gavin tried to reassure her. But Cassidy sensed something else. It was as if the animal were angry. As if it accused her of acting too rashly in her infatuation with Gavin.

"He frightens me, and...and all the same it's time I was dressing for dinner." Cassidy forced a smile at Gavin as he took her hand in his, kissing the back of it tenderly.

"You'll tell me the tale? The adventure of the mystery dinner guest? Tomorrow when we meet?" He smiled, and it warmed her.

"Yes, I'll tell you."

She turned and, lifting her skirts to her ankles, hurried toward the house. Disappointment throbbed mercilessly in Cassidy's bosom. Her first kiss was not at all as she had always imagined. She had expected to find herself near to a faint with ecstasy. Instead, she was relieved when it had ended. Disappointment had never before come so strongly to Cassidy. And now there was this mysterious dinner guest. What bend of fate awaited her in the dining hall?

❧

In dressing for dinner, Cassidy found herself primping far too long, striving all too hard for perfection in her appearance. Her hair was curled and piled perfectly on her head. A satin ecru ribbon wove itself among her locks. Long, perfectly arranged ringlets cascaded here and there down her back and over her shoulders as she tugged, dissatisfied, at the cream velvet that clung to the curve of her shoulder. Many times to many parties she'd worn velvets that were sewn to slip just off her shoulders. But this night, as she viewed herself in the glass, having donned her best gown, she was disconcerted at revealing so much of her skin. The dress was by no means inappropriately tailored, exposing only the tops of her shoulders and clavicle as it dipped into a modest V below her neck. Still, it unsettled her to see herself so mature-looking as she gazed into the glass.

The thought of poor Marietta and her ancient, rotund husband flashed before her eyes. Suddenly, she did not want to look her age. But she straightened her posture and resolved to look her best just the same, for perhaps the famous physician downstairs would see how healthy she looked, rosy cheeks and all else considered, and change his diagnosis of her ghastly disease.

"Are you quite ready, darling?" It was Ellis come to escort her down to dinner. "Or are you once again too preoccupied with that looking glass?"

Cassidy opened the door to her chamber, glaring out at her brother as he stood before her in the hallway smiling, amused with his own wit. "You beast," she scolded.

"Well, whatever it is that I am...come along or we'll be late."

Taking his arm, she mentioned, "I've not seen Mother since this morning. Or Father, for that matter."

"Well, while you were off gallivanting with your Gavin Clark, Father was locked in his study with a man whom I've never seen before, and Mother was pacing in her chamber like a caged lioness."

"What is this all about, Ellis? I've felt nervous... insecure somehow all the day long," Cassidy confided. "Something is amiss. Don't you feel it?"

Ellis, in a rare moment of somber words, admitted, "Yes. I...I don't understand their silence in the matter... Mother and Father, I mean. I...I'm unsettled myself." Then, obviously having seen her need of his strength, he smiled and added, "But look at you! How could anything unpleasant happen on this night when you look as beautiful as a young bride, radiant and ready to be presented to her bridegroom!"

"I love your flattery, Ellis, for I know that you give it sparingly and sincerely." She paused at the threshold to the dining room, lifting herself on her toes, and placed an affectionate kiss on his cheek.

"Let us sup then, sister."

He opened the dining hall doors, escorting her in to dine with their parents and the mysterious owner of the violent bay.

Cassidy smiled warmly a moment, her attention arrested by her mother, already seated at the long table laden with rich foods.

"Good evening, Mother," she greeted.

She looked up to where her father stood across the room next to their dinner guest, who turned away from the window and toward her and her brother only when her father exclaimed, "Ellis! Cassidy! At last."

Though it was her father who greeted them, it was the stranger who captured her gaze. He was indeed a stranger, a tall, dark-haired man, large in stature and astoundingly more attractive, even for his angry expression, than any man whom Cassidy had theretofore laid eyes upon. In those brief moments, Cassidy was struck by his carriage, his feature of face and form. His jaw was firmly set, masculinely squared, his cheekbones high and well defined. His mouth, though set in a rather frowning, hard expression, flaunted strong lips that were not too thin but rather perfectly chiseled. His eyes were the darkest of brown shaded by thick, black lashes, which were striking, for though his hair was dark, its shade was a hue of brown like his eyes, but lighter than his lashes and brows. His hands were clasped at his back, but it was apparent that his arms were finely and massively built, for his sleeves were fitted with an uncommon snugness just below each broad shoulder. He wore a white shirt, red cravat, black vest and coat, and black breeches, with brilliantly polished black boots that cuffed just below his knee. All this Cassidy surmised in a matter of moments, thinking that this must indeed be a highly respected and wealthy physician who stood so ominously in the family dining hall.

"Come now, Carlisle. Meet my children," Calvert Shea prodded as he put a hand at the stranger's shoulder and guided him toward Ellis and Cassidy.

"This is my son, Ellis." Ellis held out a hand, which the stranger took and shook firmly.

"Good evening, Mr. Shea," the stranger greeted. His voice was deep and rich like molasses.

"And…and this is…Cassidy, my daughter." Cassidy was unnerved by the manner in which her father stumbled over his words as if fighting not to say them. She at once, however, for propriety demanded it, held out her hand in offering that the stranger may take it and place his greeting kiss on her crocheted glove. His eyes captured her own for a moment. Cassidy again noted the odd shiver trickle down her spine, for the deep brown of his eyes held no warmth but appeared cold and indifferent.

Much to Cassidy's dismay and discomfort, the stranger paused, drawing in breath before he finally took her hand in his. Further to her dismay was the fact that his touch sent an odd spark through her arm and into her chest as he did not raise her hand to his lips but rather took the less familiar but completely proper liberty of simply placing his other hand over hers and bowing to her for an instant before releasing her altogether.

"Ellis, Cassidy...this is Mason Carlisle. Mason is a...a..." her father stammered.

"Our parents are acquainted," the stranger finished awkwardly while bestowing a rather scolding glance at Cassidy's father.

Cassidy felt that she could reach out and rub between her fingers the drapery of tension that hung oppressive in the air. Unsettled, she looked to her mother for support but found only an expression of helpless guilt on her mother's pale face.

"Come now. Let us all sit down to a satisfying meal, shall we?" Lord Calvert Shea was undone! Cassidy was in awe at his awkward manner. Restlessly he twisted the gold band at his left wrist, a gesture of uncertainty and disquiet that Cassidy had never before witnessed in her father. Glancing to Ellis, she saw the frown that threatened to show itself at any minute. Obviously Ellis was as uncomfortable as she.

As the others made to take their places, the stranger, rather Mason Carlisle, paused. Then suddenly a question erupted almost violently from him. "You've kept them in ignorance these many years?" he growled at her father.

Milady Shea dropped her gaze guiltily to her lap. Lord Shea cleared his throat and looked away when Ellis and Cassidy both looked to him for explanation. Cassidy began to tremble far more severely than before. Somehow she sensed the very fabric of her life, the security of her childhood and home, unraveling before her eyes.

"To what do you refer, sir?" Ellis asked rather too boisterously, but Cassidy was glad he had. Obviously there was something being secreted that she and Ellis needed to know.

"Sir," the man began, "I refer to the fact that neither you nor your sister have any knowledge of who I am or why I have come to Terrill."

"Should we?" Ellis was angry. It was not setting well with him that his father had kept him in ignorance about the matter.

"In my opinion...yes." The stranger's anger was increasing as well. Cassidy could see it blatantly.

"Oh, please, Mason!" her mother ventured suddenly. "We only wanted to...don't let her know this way!"

As all sets of eyes in the room fell to Cassidy, she knew then. She knew that this Mason Carlisle must be some uniquely gifted student of medicine—that he'd come to confirm her condition, whatever it was and fatal as it must be, from the looks on all their faces.

"Don't let me know what?" she managed to choke

out, forcing her head high and her back to further straighten. Always perfect posture, her mother had taught—even in the face of death.

"Oh, my darling!" Milady Shea cried out suddenly, burying her face in her hands. "We've done you such a great wrong by not telling you. We only wanted to protect you, darling. To let you lead a happy life and—"

"What are you speaking of, Mother?" Cassidy asked. "Truly you are frightening me." She felt the beginning of hysteria rising within her bosom, but it was not her mother who answered her, nor her father.

"I'm none other than he who will obviously inform you of your betrothal, Miss Shea. I'm here to bring you back to the Carlisle ancestral home for a period of adjustment before the official wedding ceremony." He was severe and heartless in his wording, blunt and lacking emotion.

Cassidy turned toward him slowly. "You…you inform me of my betrothal?" Cassidy stammered. Visions of Marietta Longswold Rapier having to endure the affections of Lord Rapier flashed horridly in Cassidy's mind. Surely not! Surely her parents would not send her off to the same fate—to wed an ancient and decrepit, obese and balding old lord in a far-off place! "My betrothal to whom?" she squeaked out.

Mason Carlisle shook his head with reproach as he glared at Cassidy's father and mumbled, "You've not prepared her in the least? Did my father know of your keeping the knowledge from her?"

Before Lord Shea could answer, Cassidy gasped,

"Your father?" All her worst visions would come true! It was clear to her now. Ellis had been right. *They'll marry you to a titled man and no other*, he'd said. Only that very day he'd said it.

An odd chuckle, a mixture of amusement and disapproval mingled, erupted from the stranger's throat. "My father?" he repeated. "Would that you were so lucky, Miss Shea," he growled, "for my father is a man above all others…but entirely obsessed with my mother. No. I am your betrothed."

Cassidy's mouth gaped open in astonishment. She looked to her father and to her mother, both of whom appeared helpless and conquered. Then she looked to Ellis, who simply stood frowning angrily at Mason Carlisle, his chest rising and falling dramatically with barely controlled anger.

"It has been thus arranged since the day of your birth over seventeen years ago. I remember that day, the day your father came to Carlisle Manor to inform my parents you had been born. The day I, at six years of age, was summoned to my father's study and notified that the babe who would one day be my wife had entered into existence."

"You are heartless in your manner!" Cassidy's mother sobbed as she stood and placed an arm about Cassidy's shoulders.

Cassidy could only stare at the man before her. Multiple visions of him were flashing in her mind. Images of his angry face before her at the altar. Images of enduring his no doubt violent physical attentions.

Images of living with a man who would loathe her for the rest of her life. She wondered fleetingly if perhaps Marietta found herself in a better lot, for it was well known that Lord Alvin Rapier, for all his unappealing physical feature, was truly and wholeheartedly smitten with his young wife. But this man—this angry, fatalistically attractive young man standing before her—wore all the signs and symptoms of complete loathing directed at the woman he had declared himself honor-bound to marry.

"It's not true what he says. It's not true, is it, Mother?" Cassidy choked out in a whisper.

"I've lived for seventeen years knowing that the choice of wife would not be my own, battling with what I wanted to do with my life and what duty and honor bound me to do. Then I come here to fulfill my duty and find that you've not even informed this child of hers!" His shouting was stinging to Cassidy's ears, and she put her hands over them, trying to drown out the sound of it.

"You will hold your tongue in my house!" Lord Shea warned.

Immediately Mason Carlisle inhaled a deep breath and fought to calm himself. "Forgive me," he forced out. And it was obvious that it was forced. "My manner was…inappropriate…in the least."

"No," Milady Shea corrected, turning toward him. "It is our manner that is inappropriate. You are obviously an honorable man, and we have failed where your parents have succeeded. I've no doubt," she continued, reaching out and placing a hand on the man's forearm, "I've no doubt that it was your mother as well as your father that so raised you to be such a man."

"They are the sole reason for my being here. For my involvement in wanting to be honorable…to perform my duty to—" he began.

"I am no one's duty, sir!" Cassidy interrupted. Her resolve to remain calm had vanished suddenly. She had meant to confront him, but when his cold, dark eyes bore into her own, she was fearful of something. Of what she wasn't quite certain, but something about this massive, attractive, and angry man frightened her. Turning back to her mother, she begged, "Please, Mother! Deliver me from this…this nightmare! This man is a stranger to me! A stranger who regards me obviously as nothing more than an hindrance. Please, Mother…I…I…"

"You will go, Cassidy." It was her father's stern voice that answered. Slowly she turned to face him, and his expression was pale and grave. He ceased in his nervous fidgeting with the gold bracelet that he ever wore and, resuming his more familiar paternal air, stated, "You will go. You know the importance…the magnitude of the importance of honor and duty. The importance of adhering to an agreement. Of—"

Cassidy could not believe what she was being told. Surely it was a nightmare! Surely she would awaken at any moment. "I am my own person, am I not?" she argued in a whisper, her voice choking with disbelieving emotion. "I...I'm not a pawn. Surely I can be allowed to choose my own way."

"Father." It was Ellis. "Surely you cannot expect Cass to go through with this?"

When her father only hung his head guiltily, Mason Carlisle spoke, still looming before Cassidy. "You may choose your own way, yes. But it would be the right thing to do to honor the agreement your parents entered into with mine. Choose your own way, and you will always harbor the knowledge of failure toward them."

His words made sense, however selfless they were. And though she had despised Mason Carlisle almost instantaneously, she pitied him for having known almost his entire life what his fate would be. Slowly she looked to her father, her mother still sobbing at her side, and spoke.

"Is this what you want, Father? For whatever reasons you have, do you want me to adhere to this betrothal agreement?"

She watched as her father's jaw clenched tightly shut. He stood erect, confident, and powerful once again. "Yes," he stated simply.

She heard her mother's somewhat heartbroken whimper and, reaching over, pulled her mother's arm from about her shoulders. "Then I will do as you wish. I will marry this man on whom I've never before laid eyes." She looked to Mason Carlisle, his eyes still heartless and dark. "This man who looks upon me as no more than a duty, one that he so obviously despises."

"I hold no grievance with you, miss," Mason Carlisle mumbled.

"None other than the grievance you hold at my ever having been born," Cassidy retorted calmly.

"Father!" Ellis was angry. It was the first time in her life that Cassidy could remember her brother shouting at their father. "This…this is insanity! She knows not of him! Nor do I! How can you ask her to…how can you expect her to do this? It is obvious he has no regard for her!"

"I have a profound regard for her!" Mason Carlisle erupted. "For I, of any in this room, acknowledge her predicament!" He stopped himself short and inhaled deeply in an attempt to regain his composure. "Excuse me. If it would be acceptable, would you have someone bring a plate to my room? It is obvious that this is the time for your family to confer alone. I've caused you enough irritation for one evening." He strode past Cassidy toward the door. The aura of power and attraction about him was undeniable. Even as he brushed Cassidy's arm in his exit, she could not deny his magnetism.

"Mason, please…" her mother began.

"Let the brute run, Mother," Ellis taunted. "The longer his filthy hands are kept from Cassidy, the better!"

Cassidy gasped as Mason paused and took hold of Ellis's lapel in a tight fist. "Only a man of honor would subject himself to such as this!" Mason growled, looking about the room and then back to Ellis in a gesture of distaste.

"Enough!" Lord Shea shouted. "Ellis! Enough. The man is innocent. Direct your anger at me if you must direct it."

Ellis still glared hatefully up at Mason, but Mason released his hold on Ellis's lapel and, tugging at his collar, said to Lady Shea, "Disregard the plate I requested." Looking to Cassidy angrily, he added, "I've lost my appetite." Then he stormed from the room, and his angry footsteps could be heard as he bounded the stairs two and three at a time.

Ellis immediately turned on his father. "What is the meaning of this, Father? Not a word! Not one inference! Never have either Cassidy or I heard of this! You've known since her birth? Known always? Today even, you knew and said nothing!" Cassidy's mother burst into tears, burying her face in her hands and collapsing into a nearby chair. "*Why*, Father?" Ellis shouted. "Why the secrecy? Why the existence of the fact itself?"

Cassidy was numb, body and mind. It was too much to take in. In the course of the past fewest of minutes, her life had been irrevocably changed. She had become a casualty like so many of her acquaintances, offered to a stranger. But for what price? What reason could her parents have for entering into such an agreement with a family of which she had never before heard mention?

"We were wrong in our silence perhaps," Lord Shea admitted, yet his authority permeated the room as he continued, "and perhaps not. For there is much that neither of you know…that neither of you could begin to understand. I only ask for your trust once more. Ever have I earned it. Throughout your entire lives I have given you no reason to doubt me…until now. With that knowledge that ever have my strivings been for your benefit…ever have I done right by the both of you…with that knowledge I tell you that still I deserve your trust. Your mother and I will regret this decision for only a short time. It will come to serve you better than you can ever imagine, Cassidy."

Cassidy felt the hot tears streaming down her lovely cheeks. Looking to her father, she could only whisper the question, "Why? Why, Father? Why me and why… why that man?"

Straightening his shoulders confidently, Lord Shea answered, "That I am not in readiness to reveal to you, my daughter. There is much that I must contemplate. Much comfort that I must give your mother. But I tell you now, with the honesty of all my heart and love for you…it will serve better than you can ever imagine."

Ellis growled angrily and stormed from the room. Cassidy dropped to her knees before her mother and, taking her hands, begged, "Who is he, Mother? This man to whom you have given me? Who is he to you?"

Cylia Shea raised her eyes to her daughter's in regained confidence. "He…he is the best of men, darling. Son to a family beloved by your father and me. He will serve you well. Believe in your father, and trust in us, please."

Cassidy stood and, turning to leave the room as well, paused, saying, "I…I want to believe in you. But it's made difficult when you will not even tell me why it is I must go with him." And she fled from the room in a torrent of tears.

ଔ

It was near to an hour that Cassidy spent alone in the west gardens sobbing as the fragrant scents of daffodil and tulip surrounded her. There was not reason to it! No way to understand it! Her parents would not even tell her how it had all come about. She could guess that they had formed a fast friendship with a couple and decided mutually that their children would wed when they were grown. But why then had she never heard the name of Carlisle before this very day?

As she thought on it, she could remember the initials D.B.C. on letters from someone to her mother. Initials of L.C. on letters to her father. Could the *C* in the initials be for Carlisle? Still, if they were such intimate friends as to wish their children to join, why then had she never heard of them? Why?

Finally, when there was no moisture left in her tired eyes for crying, she made her way back to the house. All was quiet within, as if nothing had changed. Her mother and father were nowhere to be seen, and she had heard the mad drumming of Ellis's mount leaving the stables when she had been in the garden. She knew her mind was too alive with facing the death of her independence to sleep easily.

Perhaps a book, she mused as she entered the library,

a book to divert her thoughts. But as she entered and looked toward the warming fire that crackled and spat in the large hearth, she noticed a form sitting in the deepness of a soft chair off to one side. Immediately her heart began to pound with a mania that was deafening. He sat, his elbows resting on the arms of the great chair, his hands made into tight fists, knuckles braced against one another beneath his chin. She stood frozen as he raised his eyes to her and then straightened in the chair.

"You've been found then," he mumbled. "To think they had the audacity to inquire of me about your whereabouts."

"You've known nearly your entire life?" she asked bluntly.

"I have."

"And you despised me from the first." She stated it. There was no question in her voice.

He did not argue the point—only said, "I've been sitting wondering which is the worst of it. Was it worse to know and anticipate my whole life as I have? Or would it be worse to be you and have it thrust on me unexpectedly, unwelcomely, all at once?"

"My father must have an immense regard for your father," was all she could say.

"Hmm," he mused, sarcastically somehow. "Yes, for my father."

She did not miss the insinuation in his voice. "Our mothers then."

"Ah, yes. Our mothers are great friends!" he exclaimed, and she sensed the anger rising in him once more. "And therefore, that fact alone makes this all dandy, doesn't it?"

"Are you as violent a man as you appear to be?" she asked forthrightly.

"I am," came his uncompromising response.

"Is your hatred for me as complete as it seems?"

"No."

She was somewhat astonished at his answer. "Why not?" She was again surprised at her own bold question. She shifted uncomfortably as he stood, strode toward her, and seemed to study her carefully from head to toe.

"You are, at least, a comely girl," he said rather indifferently.

She was infuriated at his brazen and worldly response. How dare he imply that her physical appearance would make the situation endurable for him? But she would not let him have the upper hand, and she quickly retorted, "And you are, at least, uniquely handsome." Then, unable to hold her tongue any further, she added, "Though...I must tell you now that it would make no difference to me were you elderly, obese, and heinous to look upon."

"Humph," he sneered rather mockingly. "You'll come to know the intense untruth of that remark." Rising from his chair and pushing past her, he strode angrily from the room.

ABOUT THE AUTHOR

Marcia Lynn McClure's intoxicating succession of novels, novellas, and e-books—including *The Visions of Ransom Lake*, *A Crimson Frost*, *The Pirate Ruse*, and most recently *The Chimney Sweep Charm*—has established her as one of the most favored and engaging authors of true romance. Her unprecedented forte in weaving captivating stories of western, medieval, regency, and contemporary amour void of brusque intimacy has earned her the title "The Queen of Kissing."

Marcia, who was born in Albuquerque, New Mexico, has spent her life intrigued with people, history, love, and romance. A wife, mother, grandmother, family historian, poet, and author, Marcia Lynn McClure spins her tales of splendor for the sake of offering respite through the beauty, mirth, and delight of a worthwhile and wonderful story.

BIBLIOGRAPHY

Beneath the Honeysuckle Vine
A Better Reason to Fall in Love
Born for Thorton's Sake
The Chimney Sweep Charm
A Crimson Frost
Daydreams
Desert Fire
Divine Deception
Dusty Britches
The Fragrance of her Name
The Haunting of Autumn Lake
The Heavenly Surrender
The Highwayman of Tanglewood
Kiss in the Dark
Kissing Cousins
The Light of the Lovers' Moon
Love Me
An Old-Fashioned Romance
The Pirate Ruse
The Prairie Prince
The Rogue Knight
Romantic Vignettes—The Anthology of Premiere
Novellas
Saphyre Snow
Shackles of Honor
Sudden Storms
Sweet Cherry Ray
Take a Walk With Me